side Effects

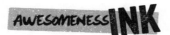

LOS ANGELES • NEW YORK

Created and produced by Running Press Kids,
an imprint of Running Press Book Publishers, Philadelphia, PA 19103

Printed in the United States of America

ISBN 978-1-941341-09-4
Library of Congress Control Number: 2014941578

10 9 8 7 6 5 4 3 2 1
Digit on the right indicates the number of this printing
09182014-C-2

Lyrics for "Sweet Little Pill" courtesy of Allison Schroeder, Ryan Shore, and Chester See (Awesomeness Music Partners, LLC).

Lyrics for "Bad Day" courtesy of Allison Schroeder, Ryan Shore, and Chester See (Awesomeness Music Partners, LLC).

Lyrics for "Boom Boom" courtesy of Allison Schroeder, Michael Corcoran, Eric Goldman, Zachary Hexum, and Niki Watkins (Awesomeness Music Partners, LLC).

Lyrics for "Pull Me Back" courtesy of Eric Goldman, Michael Corcoran, Niki Watkins, Zachary Hexum, and Allison Schroeder (Awesomeness Music Partners, LLC).

Visit awesomenessink.com

AWESOMENESS TV

side Effects

A novel by
JEN CALONITA

based on the series created by
ALLISON SCHROEDER

1 // WHITNEY

Buzz. Buzz. Buzz.

"Hello?"

"Hey, Little Orphan Whitney!" The girl's voice sounds friendly but I know it's anything but. "Put down those pills, pusher! The sun will come out tomorrow. *Not.*" I hear uproarious laughter and then a dial tone.

Outside my room, footsteps sound like a herd of elephants.

"Sam, get over here! You've got to get to bed!"

"Try and make me! I'm not tired and I'm not going to bed."

"Enough games, Sam. You're thirteen. I'm twenty-three, which means I'm in charge and I don't care if you're tired. You have school tomorrow. You have to get to sleep." Keith sounds exasperated—like he always does by this time of night.

"Sucks to be you. You'll have to catch me if you want me in my room."

They run by my door so fast, the ribbons I've won in band competitions sway on my mirror. I hear their voices echo, even though they're all the way down the hall. Our house has six bedrooms and a long, hardwood-floor hallway overlooking the downstairs. I remember a time when my brothers raced across it in their roller hockey skates. They're making so much noise tonight, I suspect Sam and Keith are in their bare feet.

Buzz. Buzz. Buzz.

My cell phone vibrates again as the shouting in the hall intensifies. I'm afraid to know who's calling me. The screen says: NO CALLER ID and when that happens, it's never a good thing.

Don't answer it. It's just the She-Bitches again, I think. *Be strong.*

But I pick up.

I try to sound upbeat. "Hello?"

"Aww, she must really need a friend." I hear one of the She-Bitches say. "She picked up on the first ring. Loser." *Click.*

The She-Bitches, as I call our school's Queen Bee and her relentless minions, hate my best friend, Susan, and me. I suspect it has something to do with the fact we're what you'd call band geeks. I guess Melanie can't handle that her new boyfriend, Scott Dwyer, used to like a dork like me.

BOOM!

I hear something slam into the wall outside my room and jump. I'd recognize Zak's crazy laugh anywhere. He's been my brother's best friend since the fifth grade, even though Zak's a year older. "Dude, I said catch!"

"You freak! Who throws balls in the house?" My older brother Jason, who's a junior, is a baseball god at our school. At least he used to be before things started falling apart.

"You're not throwing balls anywhere or catching them either." I hear Zak reply. "Try going to practice once in a while. Here! Try another one!"

I hear glass shatter and wince.

"What are you guys doing? Dad bought Mom that vase in Mexico!" I hear Keith shout. My heart sinks. I know what vase he's talking about. Mom used to collect abstract crystal vases and that pink one, shaped like a flamingo's neck, was one of her favorites. "I know I'm not Dad, but you can't keep . . ."

My phone buzzes again and I close my eyes. "Please make them stop," I whisper to myself. "Please make them all stop."

"What the hell was that?" My sister, Lexi, snaps. "I was in the middle of shaving my legs when I heard a crash and freakin' cut myself."

Buzz. Buzz. Buzz.

"Sorry we interrupted you slutting yourself up," Jason retorts. I hear a smack. "OEUF! That hurt!" As his twin, Lexi can get away with shelling out a little abuse now and then.

"If Lexi's going out, I'm going out—or at least not going to bed," Sam tries again. The youngest of my siblings is anything but the quiet one.

That would be me.

Buzz. Buzz. Buzz. They're ringing again. I might as well get this over with.

"Hello?"

"Pathetic answering for a third time, Whitney!" A new She-Bitch is on the line. "Why don't you do us all a favor and disappear like your daddy?" A group of girls bursts out laughing and hang up.

"You're not staying up, Sam!"

"What do you mean, 'slutting myself up'? How dare you say that!"

On the other side of this door, just inches from where I sit on my bed, surrounded by twinkle lights I've had strung up since Christmas, another Connolly storm is brewing. It's pretty much the same storm we've had every night since Dad left. I take that back—*before* Dad left, when Mom died. Dirty laundry is piled high in the hallways, the kitchen sink is overflowing with dirty dishes, there's crap crammed in every corner of this big, once well-taken-care-of house where Keith lives again, forced to leave medical school to take care of us. The whole situation sucks way more than I ever imagined.

As my phone starts to buzz again, I get up from my bed and walk toward the hand-painted white dresser I've had since I was five. Ditto the dollhouse Mom lovingly decorated for me that still sits on it. I can't part with it, just like I can't part with this family, however warped it's become.

I open my top drawer and take out the orange bottle with the white security cap and smile just a little when I read the medication's warning label. SIDE EFFECTS: MAY CAUSE MUSICAL HALLUCINATIONS. I open the bottle and pop one blue-and-white capsule into my mouth and swallow. I close my eyes and wait.

When I open my eyes again, the world is as it should be, shrouded in a rainbow of colors that make everything just a little bit brighter and cheerier like that scene in *Mary Poppins* when Bert and Mary jump through the painting. (Mom and I watched that movie at least fifteen times together. Probably fifteen more when she was going through chemo.) The best part of the hallucinations, though, is the singing. No more shouting. No more name-calling. Life becomes my own personal music video.

"I walk these halls as the lights go out," I sing. "Each night the same. I think I'm going insane."

I stare into the floor-length mirror in my room and a more confident me stares back. Gone are the jeans I've had for two years and the faded blue sweatshirt that has seen better days. My new ensemble is straight from *Vogue*. My long, curly hair looks shiny rather than unruly and my eyes and olive skin that I got courtesy of my South Pacific/Asian mother and Caucasian dad suddenly seem exotic. The "new" me isn't just a band geek. I can actually sing, as can the rest of my family and friends.

"We're falling apart, can't bear to be real, something inside us filled with such fear," I sing. "It would hurt too much to admit he left. What's wrong with us? Why can't we forget? Sweet little pill, take me away. Make me hallucinate, I just can't stay." The sounds in the hall fade away, and it's just me in my own happy world.

I fought Keith when he took me to the doctor. The last thing I wanted was to be on "meds." I thought medication meant I needed a straitjacket or the loony bin, but my psychiatrist, Dr. Martin, said the pills would help me cope with a mom who had been sick for too long and a dad who up and left us in the middle of the night. Paxil made me loopy. Cymbalta made me want to Hulk out. But this new one, which seems to turn my most stressful moments into musical numbers, I can handle. That's why I haven't told anyone about the side effects. Who doesn't want life to feel like an episode of *Glee*?

"Sweet little pill, take me away," the me in the mirror sings. "Falling apart at the end of the day."

I open the door just a crack and instead of fighting, my brothers, sister, and Zak are singing too. This house, which used to look like it belonged in a Pottery Barn catalog, is exactly that way again. The laundry has disappeared. Couch cushions aren't stained or missing. Mom's vase isn't broken; late bills and final notices aren't lying on an antique hall table. Maybe if I sing hard enough, Dad will be back downstairs in our chef's kitchen, flipping homemade pancakes.

Buzz. Buzz. Buzz.

When my phone vibrates again, a dose of reality takes over. When I see the caller ID, I pick up immediately. I throw myself back on my bed and hug the turquoise pillow that doubles as my teddy bear. "Hey!"

"Did the She-Bitches call you too?" Susan sounds as tightly wound as I felt a few minutes ago. Melanie's crew are banshees dressed in J.Crew. It's not a pretty combo. "Tonight they seemed obsessed with my boobs—or lack thereof."

I sigh. "They called me a pill popper and wished I'd vanish like my dad." I twirl a loose thread from my turquoise-and-white zebra print comforter around my pinkie finger and stare at the lights strung along my ceiling. "Tell me again why people call high school the best time of our lives? Ninth grade blows."

"I couldn't agree more," she says. Then she's silent for a moment. "Whit? Promise me you won't call your dad again. Calling him will only make you feel worse."

"I know," I say. But I don't really mean it.

"He's been gone for six months and hasn't tried to reach

you guys once," Susan reminds me. "Leaving yet another message is going to make you go postal."

I wince. Susan means well, but the Dad topic is still a thorny one.

"Sam?" Keith's voice travels from the other end of the hallway, probably near my parents' master suite that's closed up like a tomb. "Wherever you are, get to bed. Now!"

"Fine," Sam says wearily, finally tired of fighting. "I'll go. Night."

"Jason, privacy please?"

"From what I've heard, Lexi, you're anything but the private type," Jason says. Lexi hits him again.

"Geez, is that any way to talk to your sister?" Zak asks.

"Shut up, Zak!" they say in unison as the twins sometimes do. Zak is always here these days. He's like an unofficial sixth sibling, which is an odd thing to say when I think of how much he flirts with Lexi.

Several doors slam and then the house is as quiet as I've heard it all night. My body relaxes.

"I can't help myself," I say. "If he doesn't come back soon, we're toast. Just like my self-esteem."

"Pick it up off the floor and get some sleep," Susan commands. "I'll see you in the morning for band."

I hang up and stare at the phone in my hand contemplating what to do. *Call again. Don't call.* I feel like I have both an angel and devil on my shoulder. I turn to my side and stare at the picture of my parents on their wedding day. My mother's hair is windswept, and the lei she's wearing is blowing in the Honolulu breeze. They got married on the beach, just the two of them. Maybe that's why they look so happy. "You look just like your mom," I can hear Dad tell me. He said that the night I found him in the garden looking at a box of pictures from all our vacations, sports games . . . basically any and all of our happier moments. Mom always said she was going to put those pictures in albums, but in the end she never had a chance. "I miss those days," I remember him saying as he stared at a picture of all of us at Emmet State Park where we went camping every summer. "I'd give anything to get them back."

I hit REDIAL on my phone and listen to it ring. As suspected the voice mail picks up. "Hi, you've reached David Connolly. Please leave a message."

"Dad, this is like the hundredth message I've left you," I say, hating how desperate I sound. "Where are you? You have to come back. Keith had to leave med school, Jason hasn't hit a baseball all season, Sam is being, well, Sam, and Lexi is going for a new title—Bimbo of the Year. You said that night that you were just . . . well, you know what you said. Just get back here. Please."

BEEP! "This voice mailbox is full," a computerized voice tells me.

I throw my phone down in disgust. Through the vent in my room, I can hear Keith talking to someone that's definitely not my sister. The next sounds are ones I definitely want to block from my mind. I close my eyes and every color of the rainbow stares back at me.

That's when I hear my window fly open. I open my eyes and see a guy in a ripped tee, guyliner, and various skull tattoos climbing inside. I let out an ear-piercing scream and grab my nightstand lamp as a weapon. Then I realize it's just Lexi's latest loser boyfriend, Jared.

He holds his hands up to surrender, which, knowing him, he's probably had to do several times with the cops. "Whitney, chill! Wrong window."

"*Get out of here*," I whisper loudly.

He climbs back over the ledge just as Keith busts through my door. "What happened?" he says, sounding out of breath. I notice his shirt is half-unbuttoned. "Why'd you scream?" My oldest brother, dark-haired with rings under his eyes to match, looks tired, but not *too* tired.

"Nightmare," I lie, and Keith gives me a look. I wonder why I'm covering for the new Lexi again. I guess I don't think Keith can handle any more than he already is. "Night terrors actually.

Medication side effects," I add since he doesn't seem to be buying my story. "Who's that?" I motion to the petite blonde with the pin-straight hair hovering behind him.

Keith's cheeks color. "No one. Go to sleep. I'll see you in the morning."

He shuts my door behind him. I wait till I hear him and his blonde walk down the hall and shut Keith's door before I venture out of my room. I creak down the long hallway of our home, which was once the envy of all the moms in my elementary school car pool. ("Oh, Dianne, you're so lucky your husband is in real estate and could find a steal like this in Southern California!") My dad said when he convinced my mom to buy this house right after the twins were born, it was a money pit that had to be gutted from top to bottom. Over time, this place went from a dump to the jewel of our suburban street.

I head straight to Lexi's room, which looks like a tornado destroyed a fashion warehouse. Clothes are all over the floor, her bed is a crumpled mess, papers litter her dresser and desk. The room is empty, so I try the bathroom she shares with Jason. When I hover near the door—spying, my siblings would call it—I see her getting ready to go out. She's probably meeting up with that loser Jared again. What is she thinking? Instead of stressing out, I let the side effects take over and see a comforting hallucination: Lexi rocking out to her favorite Kesha song,

"C'Mon." The only thing that would make this moment better is if my moody sister let me dance around the room with her and join her in song.

Wait a minute. This is my side effect. Within seconds, Lexi and I are both in her room, lost in the music, and singing together about how fun it would be to go out tonight and not have another care in the world.

And for a moment, I'd give anything for the hallucination to come true.

2// LEXI

"I know my sister." I hear my twin brother, Jason, warn Zak. "She's been in that bathroom over an hour trying to make herself look like someone she's not. I wouldn't bother her right now."

I'm shaving my legs in the bathroom that annoyingly joins Jason's and my rooms, pretending I can't hear their lame conversation. While Jason is a sulky mess, Keith has power issues, Sam is being an annoying thirteen year old, and Whitney needs meds to keep her from losing it, I've found a way to deal with our family's new reality.

I go out. A lot.

"Lexi is not in a good mood, man," Jason warns him again. But it's no use.

"That's how I like her," Zak replies, sauntering into the bathroom where I've got one bare leg up on the counter. Between that cocky smile of his and the way he walks into every room like he owns it, my brother's best friend drives me insane. I guess a baseball star like him can get away with that attitude. It doesn't hurt that his slightly curly, dirty-blond hair and thick eyebrows make him look like a Greek god–in–training. Tonight he's in a plain maroon tee that highlights his tan skin and black mesh shorts. Seeing his whole jock vibe and smug attitude up close makes me glad I'm not in the so-called popular crowd anymore. He's just standing there staring at me, tossing a football from hand to hand.

"Get out of here, Zak," I tell him for the umpteenth time tonight.

He puts down the football and reaches for the toothpaste on the counter, leaning in so close that he's practically on top of me. He smells like a mix of Armani cologne and mint Ice Breakers, his gum of choice. I glare at him.

"What?" He holds up his toothbrush. "I have to brush my teeth."

"Don't you have your own bathroom at home that you can use?" I throw down the cheap Bic razor that's nicked me again in disgust. Bright red blood drips down my leg and I push my already short, black robe higher to keep the blood from staining it.

Zak puts a hand to his heart and gives me those giant puppy dog eyes of his. "That really hurts, Lexi. You know I'm from a broken home."

I snort. "And this isn't one?"

"Touché," Zak says. His brown eyes take me in like I'm the freakin' Mona Lisa. I don't want to be stared at like I'm art. Especially when I've got heavy eye makeup and hair teased to look like a French poodle. It's a look a certain type of guy likes. One that isn't going to ask me a load of questions. Zak is not that guy. Jared is.

I turn on the faucet and let it spray in a zillion directions, getting Zak wet, and making his lock on me and my body break. This is the one benefit of having a faucet on the fritz that we can't afford to fix.

Zak sticks a hand in the water and splashes it up in my direction. The cold water makes me screech. He laughs like a hyena. "You're such a Neanderthal!"

"Nice underpants," Zak says and drops his toothbrush back in the holder. I know he's pleased with himself for getting a rise out of me.

I didn't realize we had an audience. Jason is leaning in the doorway watching us. Taller than me, with wavy, jet-black hair and tan skin, my brother could get any girl in our school. His baseball stats only sweeten the whole package. (Or at least they did. I overheard one of his teammates talking in the hall the other day about how the coach might bench him for not showing up to practices. But I don't really care. That's his choice.) Jason's wearing an orange T-shirt that says: HOMEWORK: JUST SAY NO. Figures.

"Neanderthal, huh? That's a big word, Lexi," Jason teases me as Zak walks past him into Jason's room. "I thought you gave up being smart for being slutty."

"Ouch!" Zak says.

"You guys are such pigs!" I throw my shave gel can at him.

He catches it. "We're pigs?" Jason raises an eyebrow. "You're the one who has the room that looks like a sty."

"It's a work in progress," I say defensively. "At least it doesn't smell like sweat and jock straps."

Jason ignores me. "You crashing here tonight?" I hear him ask Zak as he throws himself on Jason's lower bunk.

"You have to ask?" Zak says as Jason slams the door to the bathroom. Seconds later, loud rock music fills their room.

I hate that we share a bathroom more than ever now that Zak practically lives with us. A constant reminder of the "popular" existence I no longer have.

I'm the one who wanted it that way. I dropped debate, flunked my way out of AP English on purpose (Um, who doesn't get the real meaning behind Thornton Wilder's *Our Town*?), and quit the drama club. But still, having Zak around reminds me of everything I gave up to avoid being asked things I didn't have the answers for.

"Where's your dad?"

"Is your older brother really watching you guys?"

"Are you going to lose your house? Wind up in foster care? Be on the streets?"

No, I don't want to be pretty. I don't want to be smart, and when I dress and act like I don't give a damn, that happens.

Kiss me, love me, use me, need me, take what you get. That's my new motto.

Whitney may need a pill to make her cope. I just need Jared to make me feel wanted. Fooling around is a great distraction from this life.

I walk into my room to find my leggings that have more slits in them than seams. They could be anywhere in this sty, as Jason calls it. My twin is one to talk. At least I semidecorated. If Mom was still alive, or Dad was here, I'd never be able to get away with racks of clothes in the middle of my room, large fashion prints taped to my walls with pink duct tape, or wall-size posters that say things like: DON'T HOLD BACK.

But she's not here to see it and neither is Dad.

No parental units around is good for a lot of things. Having money isn't one of them. Gone are the Anthropologie and American Eagle my friends and I adored. I traded that whole look in for clothes from Thread Bare, that little thrift store on Melrose. Their clothes get me into clubs and bars that take fake IDs. I find the leggings and slip them on, throw a pair of micro-mini jean shorts over them and add a leopard print tank. Now if only I knew where my denim jacket was. I start scanning the racks.

I hear my window open and see Jared climbing inside. "Hey, babe."

I resist the urge to cringe. The old Lexi would have given

him a lecture about the word *babe*. The new Lexi doesn't care what he calls her.

Jared wastes no time moving across the room to me, stepping on my French book, a silver miniskirt that's been on my floor for days and this month's *Elle*. His hands are on my body in seconds, and his fingers find his way under my black tank top. He kisses me hard and begins backing me toward my unmade bed. I don't push him away.

"God, I just covered for you!"

We stop kissing and look up. Whitney stands in my doorway with a look of such disappointment and disgust on her face that I momentarily feel guilty. "I'll meet you outside," I murmur to Jared.

He huffs. "Fine. But don't take long. I'm only waiting in the car for five minutes." He goes back out the way he came in, which is fine. If Keith knew I was hanging out with a kid who had been arrested twice for breaking into cars, the argument that came next wouldn't be pretty.

"What do you want, Whit?" I stare into my pink vanity mirror and apply my third layer of mascara. My younger brother, Sam, likes to call my new makeup look "raccoon eyes." I've outlined both my upper and lower lids with a thick rim of smoky black and gray liner. My pink lips are practically nude. I skip the perfume. Scents are for amateurs. I'm pretty clear in all departments what I'm looking for. "I'm on my way out."

Whitney walks in anyway, so tentative that she reminds me of a baby deer. She leans on one of my crammed racks of clothes. "Where? That house party on Wyatt Street?"

I look at her curiously. "How'd you know about that?"

Her brown eyes focus on my scratched-up floor. "People don't watch what they say around me. It's not like I'm going to get invited."

I search through the rack she's standing near for my white denim jacket, find it, and slip it on. "That's pathetic." I catch a glimpse of Whit's face and instantly feel crappy again. "Maybe if you dressed a little better, you'd start getting invites."

"What's wrong with what I have on?" Whit looks down at her sweatshirt, jeans, and slip-on sneakers.

I don't think my sister has any idea how pretty she's getting. Her long, curly hair just needs a little TLC and Garnier hairspray. Her boobs are starting to come in, and she's got such a small waist, I don't know how she keeps jeans up without a belt. I'd kill to have her eyes with their slightly oval shape and the swirl of brown and hazel flecks she has in them. Whit doesn't know how to use her assets. How would she? It's not like she has Mom around like I did to help pull herself together for high school.

"You've got on something Sam should be wearing, not a ninth-grade girl." I pull a fitted black jacket off the rack and throw it at her. "Lose the sweats and add this with some cute booties, and you'll be asked to any party." She looks skeptical. "You know how to dance, right?" Another strange face. She has got to come out of her shell! I hear a new song come on the radio and I grab Whitney's hands and spin her around the room with me.

The moment reminds me of the "dance parties" Mom would have with us after dinner when we were bathed, ready for bed, had been read to, and she was out of things to do with us till Dad could come home and kiss us goodnight. We'd dance all over the living room together, taking turns picking the music. Keith would swing Whit around under her arms, while Jason was still too young to think it was weird that he tangoed with Mom. Sam was so tiny I could carry him around the room as my own personal dance partner. "More, LiLi!" he'd say, since he couldn't pronounce my name. Sometimes we'd be so sweaty afterward that Mom would complain we needed another bath. But she wasn't really mad. Unlike Dad, she always seemed cool as a cucumber. Nothing rattled her. Not even the Big C.

Having a dance party was the last thing on anyone's agenda these days. We were lucky if we even sat down at the same table for dinner. Crap, if someone even thought to make a dinner that didn't come out of a microwavable box.

God, I need a drink.

As Whitney continues to spin, I go to my dresser. I pull the silver flask full of vodka out of my drawer and take a swig. It burns going down, but I know in a few minutes, any thought of dance parties will fade away.

I hear the music stop. Whitney is holding the remote. "You know, I don't think I want to dance anymore."

A car horn honks and I know that means Jared is getting impatient. "Suit yourself." I throw the flask back in my drawer, grab my purse and heels, and head to the window. "Take the jacket with you. You should wear it to school tomorrow. And for the love of God, pair it with something other than those lame sneakers." I don't look back. I know the expression on Whitney's face will kill me.

Down the ivy-covered trestle, I go like I have so many nights before. When I reach the bottom, I run barefoot down the long, stone driveway Dad had to have, and jump into Jared's rusty-orange Camaro that's seen better days.

"About time," he says and turns up the music. "Where to? That party on Wyatt?"

I stare out the dirty dashboard window at our McMansion. The stacked stone façade, fancy shrubbery, landscape lighting, and the topiaries guarding our front door give it the illusion there's a family inside that wants to be there.

I lean against the ripped vinyl seat that always irritates my back and close my eyes. "If you want. Anywhere is better than here."

3 // WHITNEY

I fall asleep staring at my parents' wedding picture and dream I'm a guest at their wedding. I bring them a porcelain frame with roses on it as a wedding gift, which even my subconscious finds funny since I have their wedding picture in a rose-covered frame on my nightstand. Now I'm waiting on the receiving line to congratulate my parents on their wedding (again, also kind of weird).

"Whitney! So glad you could come," my mom says as she shakes my hand.

BEEP. BEEP. BEEP. I hear my alarm and try to block it out. I know I'm dreaming, but I don't care. I want to talk to my mother.

"We're glad you're here, Whitney," my dad says. "We haven't seen you in a while."

BEEP. BEEP. BEEP. No! Not yet! How could it be morning, already?

Annoyed, I roll over and get twisted in my comforter. The clock has just turned 7:00 a.m. I hit the alarm and that's when I see a pair of bespectacled brown eyes staring at me. I scream and jump up.

"Morning!" Susan is sitting on the edge of my bed, fully dressed and ready for school as if it's completely normal that I'd wake up and find her sitting there.

I throw my head back on my pillow and groan. "Why do people keep breaking into my room?" I ask myself.

Susan thrusts her iPad in my face. "This was an emergency," she says sounding serious. "It's bad. *Really* bad. Look."

I blink, adjusting my eyes to the glow of the iPad screen, and see the CHAT MUCH? app loaded with a bunch of posts. Forget Facebook and Twitter. Everyone at University High School prefers this site because it flies under the radar (which means Principal Connors hasn't found it yet and banned us from using it). That also means the posts get nasty. *Real* nasty. If Susan is showing this to me at 7:00 a.m., that can only mean one thing. "Nooo . . . me again? What did I do now?" Susan taps the post she wants me to read. "'LMAO,'" I read aloud. "'Teacher's pet Whit C. on meds, can't handle her life. Who could?' There's forty-two comments!" I freak. "Seriously?" I hand her back the iPad and pull the covers over my head. "Pretend to be Keith and call me in sick today," I mumble. "Say I'm dying of the plague."

"That's a good idea," Susan agrees. "We'll say you caught some weird, new strain of the bubonic plague."

I get why the She-Bitches are after me, but I have no idea why anyone would make fun of Susan. She's almost too good to be real. She's stuck by me through everything. When Mom got sick, she'd sit in the waiting room with me during chemo treatments. When Dad left, she helped me map out San Bernardino County in California for places we could look for him. She even had her mom make me lunch for school since Keith was too overwhelmed to remember that kids in high school, you know, need to eat. And what does she get in return for being my best friend? Picked on by the She-Bitches just for hanging out with me.

Susan squirms uncomfortably and pushes her wavy, blonde hair away from her face. "You haven't seen what Scott wrote yet."

I exhale slowly. "Spill. It's seven a.m. I don't think I have it in me to read it myself."

Susan pushes her turquoise glasses higher on her nose, which is something she only does when she's nervous. "He's a Grade A jerk. He wrote that he only pretended to like you so he could cheat off you in math."

I pull the covers over my head again and wince. Scott's words hurt much more than the She-Bitches' comments. I thought . . . okay, I know it's crazy, but I thought he liked me. You know, before he went out with Melanie. He acted like he did. Bringing me watermelon Sour Patch Kids when we were studying together because he knew they were my favorite. Texting me to see if I needed a ride that day it was practically monsooning. Lending me his sweatshirt that day I forgot a jacket. He did that all so he could cheat on me in math? That just doesn't make sense. I knew we couldn't technically be friends anymore now that he's dating Melanie, but I didn't think that meant he was going to jump on the She-Bitch band-wagon and roast me too.

"Forget the plague," I tell Susan. "Tell them I died. No, too harsh. Tell them I moved to Mongolia."

I hear a knock on my door. "Get up, Whitney," Keith says. "You've got to get ready for school."

"I'm moving to Mongolia!" I yell back.

"Interesting choice," Keith tells me through the door. "Maybe you could do that another morning. You need to go to school today." I start to protest. "Miss any more days and you'll have to repeat ninth grade."

No, thank you. "I'm up," I say, and drag myself out of bed. My feet feel like mud. It's like they already know how bad things are going to go for me the minute I leave this house. I frown at Susan. "I already know today is not going to be a good one."

She nods and puts her iPad back in her backpack. "I brought extra clothes and shampoo with me in case they try to do something in biology again." She winces. "Yesterday, it was dissection day and they put pig intestines in my ponytail."

"Eww! Okay, that image is enough to make me skip breakfast."

I walk straight to my bedroom to brush my teeth, attempt to do something with my hair, and take my meds. I forget all about Lexi's jacket that's lying on a chair in my room. The one she claims will get me invited to parties instead of being the topic of obnoxious posts on CHAT MUCH? Instead I put on a black-and-white check flannel, jeans (always), and a blue sweater. I could wear a paper bag on my head and that wouldn't help or hurt me today. My fate is already sealed. At least that's how it feels when Keith slams the door on Susan and me with barely a "have a great day" before locking it behind us.

"Sherman Avenue or Highgrove Street?" Susan asks as her eyes dart back and forth down our neatly manicured, quiet street where huge lawns are so green they're almost iridescent. We live in the Escobar Estates section of our neighborhood and Susan's house is the beautiful green one with the gazebo next door.

"Highgrove," I suggest. "More ground cover if we need to duck and roll under a bush."

Mrs. St. Peters's lawn sprinklers kick on across the street and nearly give us a heart attack.

"On second thought, let's take our new route." I grab Susan's arm and lead her across our lawn that desperately misses our old landscaper, and behind the bushes that act as a fence along a few houses.

Susan hikes her heavy, blue backpack higher on her shoulders and moans. "I hate the grass. I always step in dog poo."

"It beats being exposed." I duck down and move quickly behind a mulberry bush. I pop up at the sound of a car. It's only a UPS truck. "When I was out in the open after gym class in the locker room yesterday, I could have sworn they were taking pictures of me changing."

"Just remember if they post them, we can trace the IP address and give it to the Feds so they can arrest them. It's totally illegal," Susan says.

I love that Susan is a computer prodigy. She lives for this online game called *Virtual Dragon Slayers* and even writes her own video game programming. Now if only she was good at hacking so we could take Melanie and the She-Bitches down.

We come to the end of the bushes and both sigh when we see the road ahead of us. We're going to be moving targets when we cross the street.

"Ready?" I say.

Susan stands up straighter and plays with the buttons on her fitted white button-down. "Yeah, I mean, no one is coming, right?" She sounds nervous. "What are the chances they're going to come by at this exact moment?"

The thought makes my stomach growl. Or maybe that's because I didn't eat breakfast. "Yeah, we just need to make it to that large oak tree on the lawn over there and then we're home free till school. No one goes down that end of the block. It's a dead end." The houses on this street are so large, there's only five or six of them.

"Thank God the Jensens let us use their backyard as a cut-through," Susan says.

We both peek out from the bushes and look both ways. No cars are coming. The only sound on the street is a lawnmower several houses away and a mom trying to wrangle two angry preschoolers into her minivan to go to Trader Joe's.

"And go!" We start to run.

The sound of tires screeching makes me pause in the middle of the street.

"*No, no, no*," Susan whispers to herself, sliding her glasses higher on her nose.

I watch as Melanie's yellow Volkswagen Mini Coop convertible pulls away from the curb where it was parked and roars down the street toward us. I've got to hand it to her. Pretending to be parked on a residential street just to torture us on the way to school is a new low even for her and her minions.

Susan and I back up, stepping on the curb we thought was so safe just moments before, and watch as Melanie and her friends Julia and Arianna pull up next to us seemingly in slow-motion. They look like they just stepped out of an ad for

Kate Spade. All three of them have on the same pair of sunglasses (in different colors, of course) and are in their standard prepster uniform of tee, cardi, and skinny capris or skirts. They coordinate, but dare not match. Their clothes are so bright, it takes my eyes a minute to adjust to what I'm seeing in front of me.

Melanie throws the car in park near the curb and jumps out of her seat to sit on the ledge of the rolled-down window. Like puppets, Julia and Arianna do the same, hopping up to sit on the back of the car top to stare at us.

"Hi, girls," Melanie says in that sugary sweet voice of hers that wins over teachers and makes even the nerd quotient sometimes wonder if maybe she's not as evil as they think.

They shouldn't be fooled. She is evil.

Melanie slides her sunglasses back on her head so we can see her icy-blue eyes. I have the sudden urge to scream "don't look directly at her or you'll turn to stone!" But I don't.

"Taking a short cut today?" Melanie asks and Arianna half sneezes, half laughs. "So glad we caught you." Her eyes lock on my best friend. "Suzy-Q! Look at your hair. I'm so glad you got those nasty pig guts out of it."

"Yeah, it only took four washes." Susan instinctively touches her blonde hair, which is a much nicer shade than Melanie's—and didn't come from a bottle.

Melanie's hair is pulled back in low pigtails that reveal her oversize pink stud earrings. Julia's wearing the hoop version of them, while Arianna's are in royal blue—the same shade as Melanie's sweater that she's paired with a short, pink skirt. Julia and Arianna are both redheads. Bottle redheads. They were blonde, but I have a feeling the shade made Melanie feel competitive and Melanie never likes to be upstaged. She takes in my outfit from head to toe. "How's it going, Whit? Feeling good this morning?" This time Julia is the one who laughs. "We were looking for you so we could give our condolences on the whole Scott thing."

I hate the way Melanie speaks. Every word she says is drawn out and it makes my skin crawl.

Melanie shakes her head sadly. "It was so mean what Scott said about you on CHAT MUCH? But seriously, Whit. What would make you write him a thank-you note for Sour Patch Kids. What are you? In second grade?"

They laugh. They laugh and the sound irritates me like a nasty papercut.

"I guess you'll finally have to accept defeat and stop trying to give him math help, geek." Melanie's face hardens. "It's not like he's going to talk to you anymore." I stare at the street where a piece of gum is flattened like roadkill. "If you had wanted to keep him interested, maybe you should have gone your sister's route. At least sluts manage to keep a guy for one night."

Julia holds her arm up so Melanie can high-five her. Melanie just looks at Julia's sleeve, which has a splotch of coffee on it and ignores her. Julia slowly lowers her arm.

"Shut up," I say quietly and Susan looks at me. They *all* look at me.

Melanie's friends stop laughing. For a moment, Arianna actually seems concerned. Maybe she has some leftover sympathy for me from when we were best friends in third grade. The look is fleeting. So is Melanie's tolerance of my minor insubordination.

"What did you say to me, prude?" She leans forward and rests her hands on the dashboard window frame. I immediately clam up. "I didn't think so, loser."

Loser.

Geek.

Prude.

I throw my backpack down in disgust and hear a roar in my ears like a freight train. I know my medication's side effects are taking over the second my fingers start to tingle. The world begins to swirl around me like a tornado. When the wind dies down, I'm wearing an entirely new outfit: a fitted red leather studded jacket and a tight black dress. I glance at Susan, who's wearing a tight black tee and red skirt. She has on heavy makeup and has rock-star hair. I suspect I have the same. We both look ready for our music video close-up, which makes sense now that I see the army of cutely dressed cheerleaders behind us who are acting as backup dancers. The cheerleaders shake their red pom-poms in the air and Susan does the same. At that moment, a red guitar appears in my hands. I waste no time running at Melanie's car.

Melanie, Julia, and Arianna are frozen in time, glued to their seats and forced to watch my performance. There's an added benefit to that. Susan can seemingly draw on their faces with a nonexistent pen, scratching out their smug smiles. The first time she does it, they look horrified. They're even more so when the cheerleaders pull Melanie from the car and start pushing her around. One pulls her pigtails out.

I belt out "Mean," the Taylor Swift song that has become Susan and my anthem for dealing with the She-Bitches. My fingers fly over the guitar strings in my fingerless gloves and stack of bangles that somehow don't make me hit any wrong notes.

I rock out to my thoughts, thinking about how Melanie's words remind me of things far worse than a papercut. How they twist the knife and then leave them in, making me wish I could be anywhere but here. Their actions are like nails on a chalkboard, kicking me when I'm already down.

As Susan and the cheerleaders dance behind me, I strum my guitar and sing louder. A few of the cheerleaders get in Melanie's face and she winds up on the ground. I belt out Taylor Swift's words, thinking about how true this song is. Someday I'll be living in some amazing city like New York with a kick-ass job and Melanie will still be the same person she always was: mean.

Julia and Arianna cower in the car, which Melanie races back to, but for once I have the upper hand. And I like it. A pyrotechnic explosion timed to the cheerleaders' moves makes me strum the guitar harder. Melanie's the uncomfortable one for a change. With one last twirl of their pom-poms, the cheerleaders toss them into the air and cheer. I finish big, my chest rising up and down in excitement until . . .

The swirling starts again, the cheerleaders fade away, and I'm standing in front of Melanie's Mini Coop in my flannel T-shirt like none of that just happened. I know it didn't, but I wish it did.

"Hello?" Melanie drags out the word. "Anyone in there, Whitney? Earth to Whitney!" The girls laugh. "God, she's gone mute."

"Let's go," I tell Susan and we cross in front of their car and hurry to the other side where our security gate of manicured bushes is waiting. A landscaper looks at us sadly as he prunes a topiary shaped like the letter A.

The rest of the day doesn't go any better. They toilet-paper my locker, write *loser* on my gym locker in Sharpie, and throw a banana peel at me at lunch. I've never been so happy to go home at 3:00 p.m., even if I walk in and overhear Keith talking to Harry Freitas. He's the family lawyer, but he was also a good friend of my dad's. Today he's in a suit, which means he's all business. Never a good sign.

"Want to give me the bad news first or the really, really bad news?" I hear Keith say and I glance around the doorframe to survey the scene further. Keith stands in our large, white-washed kitchen Mom had redone only two years ago with top-of-the-line appliances. He looks scruffy and unshaven, and is wearing a fitted button-down shirt that has clearly never seen an iron. His arms are leaning on the kitchen island for support. "Just tell me, Harry. I can take it."

I can't watch this. I turn back to the hall table and start flipping through all the overdue bills. But I can't stop myself from listening in.

"I'll start with the bad news," Harry says grimly. "I petitioned to have the money in your mother's will released to you, but it's going to take some time and they won't give you access to your father's account since it's assumed he's still alive." He pauses and I can hear the whirl of the washing machine going in the laundry room grow louder and louder.

"Can't we get some sort of extension from the bank?" Keith asks. "I don't know how this works, but clearly in this situation . . ." He trails off.

"I don't think it would do you much good," Harry tells him. "The money's dried up. Your father was already six months late in payments. He was using the money for some experimental treatment for your mom."

"What you really mean is he was socking money away to start his new life without us," Keith says bitterly.

"You don't know that," Harry says quickly.

"Don't defend him!" Keith barks. "Sorry. That news just really sucked."

"Well, the really bad news is . . ." Harry hesitates. "Since you don't have the money, and clearly none is coming anytime soon, the bank has given you thirty days till they foreclose on the house."

My stomach drops to an all-time low. We're losing our house? Where are we going to live? What's going to happen to us? Will we be split up? I feel like I can't breathe.

Keith exhales slowly. "How the hell am I supposed to come up with that money?"

"Wow, this is their worst pep talk yet." I hear someone say and jump.

I turn around. Sam is lurking behind me. His light brown hair is growing longer in the front and while he's still wiry, he's seemingly shot up overnight. That explains why all his jeans have suddenly become ankle-length. I know he's thirteen, but whenever I see him, I still think of him like he's a four-year-old, begging me to read him Dr. Seuss one more time before bed.

"What are you doing here?" I hiss and hide the bills behind my back.

"Same as you," Sam says nonchalantly. "Eavesdropping." I don't say anything. He tries to get around me. "What's behind your back?" His face breaks into a mischievous grin. He lunges for my arm, but I'm too quick and I jump out of the way.

Sam accepts defeat easily. "It's pretty bad, isn't it?"

His brown eyes look so sad, I'm not sure I can lie to him.

"I don't know what you're talking about." I hear something large fall upstairs and then the sounds of Lexi and Zak arguing.

"Whitney?" Sam grabs my arm before I can leave the room. "Don't tell the others about the foreclosure," he says quietly. "They can't handle it."

He walks away, leaving me standing there holding my stomach like I've just been sucker punched. My little brother shouldn't have to know the word *foreclosure* and he shouldn't have to grow up overnight either. But he clearly is.

4 // LEXI

I'll be the first to admit it—what I'm doing right now is completely juvenile.

And fun.

Sue me for acting like a twelve-year-old for a split second.

"Get off of me!" I screech, half laughing, half yelling as I push back against Zak as he pins me to the floor and smears Elmer's Glue all over my chin.

"Nope!" Zak drips another glob of glue onto my cheek and I shriek. "I vote we papier-mâché you instead of doing a diorama on the Panama Canal. We'd definitely get an A. Watch out, Athena," he crows. "Lexi Connolly is the real statue in town!"

I laugh and rub my glue-covered cheek against his. "You're such a freak." I stop struggling. Zak stops holding me down. The two of us stare at each other intently. I'm clearly aware of his chest rising and falling against my own. Up close, I can see how bad he needs a shave, not that I mind the stubble. I've also never noticed that dimple on his right cheek before. "Freak," I say again softly because I have to say something. Anything. Because if we don't, we just might lean closer and . . .

"Are you two okay?" Whitney asks as my door flies open. Her concern quickly turns to amusement when she sees our compromising position and our half-done diorama lying on the floor.

Zak and I separate as if the two of us are on fire. I take his hand and let him pull me up—then shove him away. He pretends to be wounded.

"No!" I quickly fix my hair, which is out of whack after our miniwrestling match. "He's demonic! And he's going to get us a D on this project all because he never learned how to use glue in kindergarten."

"Me?" Zak acts outraged and pulls on his faded blue T-shirt. "You're the one who doesn't know an intro from a conclusion."

"What?" I cry. "I'm the one who wrote the entire report!"

"You did?" Zak scratches his head and looks around my disheveled room. He moves a stack of magazines, tosses a cotton candy pink lace bra without barely glancing at how sexy it is, and zones in on my oversize, slouchy bag. "Where could it be? Did you stash it in here?"

"No!" I lunge for the bag and he holds me back with one defined arm while Whitney stands in the doorway and watches. She's such a future Fed or a TMZ reporter. I'm not sure which. "Give that back!"

I'm such I fool, I don't even remember what I stashed in that bag until Zak unzips my secret compartment and pulls out a tampon and my birth control pills. The smile on his face vanishes. Whitney looks like she wants to fall through the floor. "Look at you being all prepared for any situation," he says, but his voice is anything but playful now. "How's it going with that asshole you're dating anyway? Is Jared still cheating on you?"

I rip the bag and its contents out of his hands. Zak is such an ass. I don't want him to know my business. I don't want him to know anything about Jared. Why does he care so much? "God, I hate you."

Zak raises an eyebrow. "Oh, now you hate me?" He moves closer and I step back, wondering what he's doing. "Because a minute ago it seemed like you felt differently. You're so hot and cold with me that it's insane. Maybe you should finish the project on your own." He shakes his head and starts walking out of my room.

Why does he have to make things more complicated than they need to be? "Stop," I say, trying not to sound as bothered as I really feel. "Let's just get this project over with."

Zak walks back over and stops inches from my face. He lifts his hand and I think he's going to pull me in for a kiss. Instead he wipes the glue off my cheek. "Fine. Let's get back to work," he repeats quietly.

"Um, guys?" Whitney's meek voice breaks the awkward silence. She shifts uncomfortably and stares at her sneakers. Why hasn't she taken my advice and ditched them? Me, I'm in leggings with knee pads, short shorts, and my white denim jacket. That coat is quickly becoming my fashion staple. "Keith just called for a family powwow in the kitchen. Five p.m. And, Zak? While you're practically family, I don't think he meant you had to be there too."

Zak runs a hand through his mop top. He still seems a little off his game after what just happened. "No problem, Whit. I've got my own family misery to attend to. I've got to go home and make sure my parents haven't tried to kill each other."

None of us laugh.

I'm too busy thinking of this mandatory family meeting Keith has called. Getting the five Connolly kids in the same room these days is an anomaly. Keith's got his hands full with legal stuff, Sam acting out, and Whit and her meds, which is great in a way because Jason and I have pretty much been able to fly under the radar. Something pretty major must have happened for him to want us all to convene at the same time today. My mind immediately thinks the worst: they've found Dad and he's already got a new family in New Mexico that he'd rather be with.

When I walk downstairs a few minutes later, Whitney is straining spaghetti in the sink while Sam sets the table in the unused dining room. I hate staring at that mission-style table Mom and Dad bought instead of a hot tub. It reminds me of all the parties the two of them used to throw. Elaborate ones with waitstaff and rented china. Those days are gone. Today Keith is stirring sauce on the stove while he talks on the phone. Probably another bill collector. I've stopped answering the house phone at all when I see an 800 number, but Keith keeps trying to give these guys our pathetic story as if they're going to feel bad for us and wipe our bills clean. They don't.

"Thanks for calling." I hear Keith say. "I really appreciate it."

He looks up from the sauce and stares at Jason and me who have walked in at the same time. We both lean against the doorframe. Neither of us makes a move toward the table to help Sam finish putting out all the forks and cups. I think that's because my twin and I are both in agreement that a family dinner is the last thing either of us wants to sit through. I'd rather get my tongue pierced. Actually that's not such a bad idea.

"Glad you two could grace us with your presence for a change," Keith adds. I cross my arms and look away while Jason huffs. "Want to know who I was just on the phone with, Jason? Your coach just chewed me out for your lack of participation this season. Apparently you've decided baseball practice is optional."

"We're having a difference of opinion," Jason says unapologetically. "He thinks some freshman's curveball is better than mine. I think he's an asshole."

"Mouth!" Keith says, glancing at Sam, who seems to enjoy being off the chopping block as much as I am. Whitney looks anxious. "We'll come back to you. First, I've got a bone to pick with Lexi."

Here we go.

"Apparently you've skipped so many days this semester that you may not pass." Keith mockingly applauds us. "Nice job, guys."

I feel a flash of anger at how he's talking to us. It certainly isn't parental, if that's what he's going for. "You're one to talk. I don't remember you being a model student in high school."

"Actually, I came pretty close compared to you two," Keith shoots back. "I didn't lose my scholarship and didn't flunk out, so yeah, I win this one. Now sit down. We're eating."

"I'm not hungry," I say and prepare to ditch this lame party.

"I said '*sit down*'!" Keith yells at the top of his lungs.

We all freeze and look at him. I've never seen my brother melt down like that before. He wasn't this upset his first night home from UC San Diego midsemester. When Harry Freitas told him he'd have to stay till Dad got back or risk us going into foster care, Keith didn't even tear up.

I do as I'm told and sit. We all do. We just don't know what to do next. Keith brings over the spaghetti. He's poured jarred sauce on it. A sad-looking bag of salad sits in the middle of the table alongside a value bottle of dressing. At least he didn't try to go all healthy and try to get us to drink milk. He's put out two bottles of soda and a pitcher of water. Sam taps his empty glass with a fork while Whitney keeps rearranging her silverware. Jason tears his napkin into little pieces. Keith stares at his empty plate like he's forgotten Mom and Dad aren't here to do the serving. Do you want to know the saddest part about this family dinner?

We don't even know how to have a normal conversation anymore.

5 // WHITNEY

The air at the table feels static and thick like it is does right before a thunderstorm rolls in. We Connollys never have family dinners anymore and it doesn't take a session with my psychiatrist to understand why.

I remember the night Keith came home from medical school six months ago like it was yesterday. He took us to Chili's to drop the bombshell Harry Freitas told him: Four kids under eighteen couldn't live in a house without an adult present and Dad had been MIA for a week at that point. Keith said he was going to stick around to take care of things till Dad got back. I haven't been able to look at cheese fries the same way since.

These days it's rare we sit down to eat together. When we do, it usually only takes about two minutes before we look like we belong in a WWE Wrestling match. Lexi and Jason are always pulling Keith in to the ring for a battle royale.

And I have always played the part of referee. "Guys, the pasta is getting cold," I say as we feel the aftershocks of Keith's explosion.

No one answers me. I look from Keith to Jason, Lexi, and then Sam. Everyone is staring at their red plastic Solo plates that have become our family's china. My heart thumps hard and fast in my chest, and I wait to see who's going to abandon ship first this time. Jason's long brown hair hangs in his face, hiding him away from us. Sam might crawl under the table and overturn the whole thing on us. Lexi keeps running her fingers through her hair, her midnight-black nails blending into her curls. Keith seems the worst. His stubble is thicker, the sleeves on his gray shirt are rolled up like he's been hard at work and getting nothing done, and I can practically see lightning bolts shooting out of his head. As I feel another hallucination taking over, I pray they all stay here long enough for me to have one.

I tap my water glass and it makes a tiny *ping*. The room feels dark and I remember no one bothered to turn on anything other than wall sconces that surround a watercolor painting Sam did for Mom in fifth grade of a bowl of fruit. Sam taps his plastic cup of milk along with me and the drink shakes so much it might splash over the rim. Jason uses the table like a drum and Lexi holds her fork and knife as drumsticks. Lightning flashes in the room. The storm is here.

"It's been a bad day," I imagine Keith singing, his voice broken.

"A really, really bad day," Lexi sings softly, staring at the embroidery on the flowery table runner Mom inherited from

Dad's mom when they were first married.

"A kick-you-in-your-balls kind of day," my brother Jason agrees in song.

"I lied," I sing, staring at the cuckoo clock on the far wall near a fireplace that hasn't been lit in years.

"I cried," Lexi admits.

"I was paralyzed," Sam belts out and I feel even sadder.

The side effects make me feel stronger, making me admit things I'd never fess up to in song. I stand up. "I made this mess."

"I had one worse," Jason tells us.

"Just open up," Keith begs him, but Jason turns to Lexi.

"Scream, shout, and curse!" she shouts lyrically.

I watch Jason put his hand on Lexi's shoulder. "You're just like Mom," he sings. "You act so strong."

Lexi looks away. "And she was barely holding on."

Jason's voice is barely audible. "Wish I was gone."

Lexi agrees with him. "Gone."

This time, we all leave the table, but we don't go far. I imagine us playing a game of musical chairs. The storm rages, the lightning flashes, and we're each locked in our own private hell, allowing our demons to come to the surface for a change. I picture a wall of family photographs behind us, all in silhouette.

"You think you've had a bad day? Think you had it rough?" We sing as we round the table. Our voices grow angrier and louder as we move. "I've taken all I can. Now I've had enough."

I may be the only one on meds, but the window to my siblings' souls makes me suddenly see how damaged they all really are. Lexi and Jason, who used to be so close, are gunning for each other. They're blaming each other for not being real when the truth is neither of them are anymore. Sam doesn't want to be a ghost.

Standing there in a blue tee that's too big on him and was obviously stolen from Jason's closet, he looks ten. "Hey, I'm right here," he sings, inserting himself between Lexi and Jason who are arguing so badly in song in my mind they're overturning chairs. "Nobody cares I'm in eighth grade and I've got new body hair."

Lexi holds up her hand. She definitely doesn't want to hear about that. Jason, though, understands where he's coming from, so I turn to Keith, so lost in his own thoughts.

"Tell the truth," I beg, singing just to him.

Sam joins me. "It's time they knew. If you don't tell them, I'm going to."

"We lost the house," Keith finally sings mournfully.

In my mind, the song seems to stop and the pictures I imagined start crashing to the floor. Lightning illuminates Lexi and Jason's reaction. The bottom has fallen out from under us and there's no escaping the reality anymore.

"It's not my fault," Keith tries to explain.

But no one will listen. The storm can't be stopped. Dinner together can't hide what we really feel. In anger, we begin destroying anything and everything in our path. Tonight that means salad and spaghetti. As the storm rages, so does our food fight. Milk splashes over the side of the table. Glass shatters. Tomato sauce splatters onto the cream-colored walls.

"Lost the house," Jason cries in song. "God, we're so lost. I blame you!" he tells Keith.

"You, you, you!" Lexi agrees, and sits down on the table to hold her head in her hands.

"I'm right here!" Sam jumps up on the table, and Keith tries to pull him down. It doesn't work. "Listen up!"

"I made this mess." My voice is quieter than the rest, but then when I see how enraged they are, I feel like I'm going to really lose it. The hallucinations aren't enough to hide the truth. I have to finally let it out. "ENOUGH!" I cry and the music grinds to a halt.

Everyone is sitting where they should be. Spaghetti isn't dripping from the walls.

"This is all my fault," I say, my voice wavering, but I know if I don't say this now, I never will. They're all staring at me. "Dad told me he was leaving and I let him go."

Everyone starts talking over each other at once. Keith shushes them.

"What?" Keith's hushed voice tells me he doesn't believe what he's hearing.

Sometimes I still can't believe it either.

"I thought he meant he was just getting out of here for a few days, to clear his head," I explain, the words coming quicker than I can get them out. I can't handle the way they're staring at me, Lexi's nude lips curled into a frown so deep, I'm afraid she's morphed into the Joker. Sometimes her makeup looks like she intended it that way. I can't stay at this table any longer. "But I think I know where he went," I add and bust out the French doors behind me into the backyard. The sun has set by now, but the air is still warm. A cicada calls out in the distance. I don't stop till I've reached the pool house where I've stashed the wooden box. Clutching it, my brothers and sister join me on the patio and Keith flips on the outside lights. The pool lights go on and I look at the calm, clear water hoping it will give me the strength to tell my brothers and sister what I've been hiding for six months now. It's been eating me alive and I can't hold back anymore. I sit down on one of the stone ledges that surround the overgrown garden where bushes need pruning and pieces of lawn furniture left uncovered are starting to rust.

Keith, Jason, Lexi, and Sam stand around me, waiting for me to explain myself. I open the box and stare at the first picture. It's one of us as a family—Mom and Dad included—standing with Jason after his team won a division title and went on to the California state championships. We look so happy. I think that's what was so hard for Dad. We were happy once.

"A few weeks after Mom's funeral, I found Dad out here looking through the pictures in this box," I explain. "Baby pictures, family vacations, barbeques with Grammy and Gramps, ones with Mom before she got sick. He said it was hard for him to look at the past without being jealous of it. I told him it was hard for me to think of those times too, but that didn't seem to make him feel any better."

"I'm not doing a very good job, kiddo," he said to me as he flipped through the pictures in the box. His face was haggard. His clothes were hanging off him. I think he'd been wearing the same blue-and-white striped shirt and jeans two days in a row. His graying hair hadn't seen a comb, which was funny considering how much we all teased him about his "Realtor hair." He wore custom suits that he swore to Mom helped him seal the deal when he was selling a house. Not anymore. "I'm failing you guys here."

"Don't say that," I remember telling him. I stared into his brown eyes that mirrored Keith's and lied to his face for the first time ever. "We'll be okay."

I knew he didn't believe me. I didn't believe it myself either.

"I can't stand seeing you all so sad, not sleeping, walking around like zombies," he said. "It's killing me. I'm not sleeping."

He ran a hand through his messy hair. "I can't stay in your mother's and my room anymore. I can't sleep there without her. I promised your mom . . ." I perk up, but he trails off. "Never mind." He stood up and handed me the box. I didn't get what was happening. He motioned to the pictures in my hand. "That seems like a lifetime ago." His voice cracked. "I'm no good to you kids right now and until I am . . ." He paused like he was trying to find the words or maybe understand what he wanted. I don't think he knew. "I need to figure some things out first. Okay, kiddo?" He touches my cheek and I just nodded, but I didn't understand.

"He wasn't making a lot of sense," I tell the others. "When he left, I thought he was just taking a drive or something." I feel my voice rising. "I didn't realize he was leaving for good." They're all just staring at me, and I sense I'm losing them. They don't understand what happened that night. They don't get that I was scared and had no clue what to tell my dad who was supposed to have all the answers. "If I had, I would have stopped him."

They remain quiet. The only sound is the symphony of cicadas who have joined us in the yard to sing their song. There's no singing in my family, however much I wish another hallucination would pull me from this moment and wash it all away.

"You've got to be kidding me," Lexi says, sounding stunned. "No wonder we had to medicate you, you freak. You let him leave us!"

"I didn't mean to," I try to explain, but Lexi just holds her hand up for me to stop.

"I'm outta here," she says and walks away.

Jason gives me a look that could wound a puppy. "Me too."

All that's left is Keith and Sam. My younger brother picks up the box I've set beside me and opens it. I watch him silently flip through pictures, stopping at one of him with Dad at his communion. He's the only one who hasn't said anything to me yet. Then I remember Keith is still standing there.

"I'm so sorry," I say, hoping he of all people will understand. He's the adult here now. He'll get what happened and tell me it's okay, that I didn't know what was going on, like Mom would have.

But I'm wrong. "How could you keep this from us?" Keith asks, his voice reminding me of shattered glass. "Now it's too late to do anything."

He disappears into the darkness and any hope I had left vanishes along with him.

6// ZAK

Jason and I joke I have more of my crap at his house than I do at my own. I've never been able to stay away from the Connollys. What's not to love about a family that genuinely likes each other? My parents have hated each for years, which explains why I'm an only child. To them, I'm a blemish on their tax returns that they need to shell out college money for.

Mr. Connolly was more of a dad to me than my old man was. I met him when he coached Jason and me in Little League. Jason and I were best friends by the third game of the season, so I was over their house a lot from the beginning. It was Jason's dad who taught me how to hit a curveball. He showed us how to handle a pop-up fly and explained the art of stealing a base. He'd hit Jason and me ball after ball in their backyard till we begged him to take a breather.

"You think Clayton Kershaw asked his dad for a break?" Mr. Connolly would say. "Get back out there."

I think he liked playing ball with us as much as we liked hanging out with him. Keith had quit ball years ago, and Sam had zero interest in sports. He, Lexi, and Whitney were more like their mom, into the arts and theater and shit. While they'd be off looking at some new exhibit at the Getty Center, we'd be outside having batting practice. Then Mrs. Connolly would come home with fresh fish and all these organic sides from the farmers' market and say, "You're staying for dinner, right, Zak?" like it was a given and it was.

It sucked what happened to them.

Kids at school were divided into two camps when it came to the Connollys. Sure, everyone felt bad when their mom died. Mrs. Connolly was always up at school running some crappy PTA fundraiser or cheering us on at ballgames. People liked Mr. Connolly too, but when he disappeared one day, it was like El Niño blew in. All anyone wanted to do was talk trash about them now because they were the gossip item du jour. Lexi, Whitney, and Jason weren't morons. They heard the talk in the hallways. Some people said David Connolly got in over his head flipping houses, screwed over some investors, and ducked out of town in the middle of the night. Others went with the old standby—he had another family in New Mexico. And the third kind thought they had it all figured out—he blew his money on chemo treatments for his dying wife and they couldn't even afford the mortgage on their house anymore.

Bingo. Jason had said as much. That lawyer guy was always sniffing around, bringing nothing but bad news. I knew one day

I would drive over and see a foreclosure notice on their front door. But it still blew. The Connollys had had their hearts ripped out and stomped on and no one was left to pick up the pieces. Keith was a decent guy, but he had a life of his own he wanted to live. Whitney broke down so bad they had to put her on meds. Sam was completely ignored. Jason hadn't struck out a batter in months. And Lexi ditched the drama club she lived for and tried burnout on for size. You could see how much it was killing her not to be part of the spring show this year. She usually hand-picked all the costumes. Every girl likes clothes. Not all of them knew how to work them like Lexi does.

That girl gets under my skin. We've been dancing around each other since her boobs came in and she discovered I had forearms. It was fun at first; the way she'd find a way to talk to me and then we'd trade wicked one-liners like we were on a late-night talk show. I knew Lexi was into me—Jason had said as much—but when her mom spiraled downhill fast and died, and her dad disappeared six months ago, things changed. *She* changed. It wasn't just the big hair and the makeup that made her sometimes look like a drag queen. She didn't care who she was anymore. "Used and abused," was how my buddy Kyle described her new motto. Lexi had become the class whore and she liked it.

While I tried to fight it, I still couldn't quit her. I guess that's why I was stoked when Mr. Hendricks assigned Lexi and me as partners on that history project. Today, when we were supposed to be gluing Popsicle sticks together to make a diorama of the Panama Canal, old Lexi came to hang for a while. And I liked it. Flirty, funny, fast with the quips, we were in a groove. We were getting someplace. Hell, when I had her pinned to the floor like that, her body under mine, I thought we were *really* getting someplace. And then Whitney walked in (the "fuzz" Jason calls her), and Lexi wigged out again, acting like I was a leper.

Her tease routine was getting as tired as Ryan Seacrest's hair on *American Idol*, so I didn't care when Whitney announced they were having a rare family dinner. I drove home and figured I'd chill there for a bit. When I showed up, Mom and Dad were icing each other out over a freaking cable bill.

"Who pays an extra nine ninety-nine a month for Netflix, Ron?" Mom was yelling like he'd just dropped a hundred bucks on lotto scratch-offs. "At least order Showtime so we can watch *Homeland*!"

"What do you care, Eileen?" My father, who didn't have a backbone till Mom broke his last year when she admitted she had an affair, roared back. "You spend more than that each morning on a latte after a hot yoga class that has done nothing to help the size of your ass!"

They had been like this as long as I could remember. If someone ever decided to do a reality show on couples who should divorce but don't and drive their families crazy, my parents would be the stars. Separate bedrooms, individual vacations (sometimes I was invited with one of them, sometimes I wasn't), and divided living spaces. The kitchen had become the only neutral territory (my mother even claimed the mud room, even though that was technically mine since it was filled with my baseball gear and nine hundred pairs of cleats). They were standing at opposite ends of the marble top kitchen island fighting over nine dollars and ninety-nine cents.

I swiped an apple out of the bowl on the island and watched their barbs fly back and forth like it was an Xbox 360 game. Mom barely looked up and acknowledged me before she started waving a spatula in Dad's face. Dad stopped for a moment, though.

"Did Coach say you're starting this weekend?"

"Yeah," I said. That was more than I'd said to him in two days.

"Good," he grumbled and his gray eyes focused back in on my mom. "Maybe if you were actually home some nights, Eileen, I wouldn't have to watch lame movies on Netflix."

I left them like that in the kitchen, went upstairs to shower, than dumped some more clothes in a bag to bring back to Jason's. If I was lucky, I wouldn't have to make an appearance again till at least Monday. I couldn't show up back at Jason's yet. It had only been an hour so I decided to hit that party Ryan Weiss was throwing while his parents were in Maui. But by the time I got there, people were already puking into the pool. There's nothing like a sloppy girl slurring in your face to sober you up. I saw that loser Lexi's been banging too. That class act yakked into a rose bush, then turned around and pinched some girl's ass.

I'd seen enough. By that point it had been three hours. Connolly family time had to be over by now. When I pulled into their long driveway, I found Lexi and Jason arguing over the car keys.

"Give them to me!" Lexi was fired up. Nothing new there. "I've gotta meet up with Jared."

"No way! It's my car." Jason held the keys over his head and Lexi reached for them, her long legs bare except for those strange high socks and knee pads, stretched out to grab them. Those white shorts barely covered her ass. Then I noticed the black tank top. Don't get me wrong. She looked good. She just wasn't trying to look good for me.

"What's going on?" I played referee with these two a lot.

"Oh good, Zak's here." Lexi sounded ticked off. "Let him take you wherever you want to go. I need the car."

Her makeup streaked down her cheeks like she'd been crying. Jason looked sort of out of it too. What the hell had happened now?

Lexi jumped for the keys again, missed, and screamed in aggravation. "Just give them to me, jerk," she said and pushed him hard.

She was going to crack the car up if he gave her the keys. "I'll drive you," I told her and she looked intrigued. "Anywhere but to see Jared." She rolled her eyes and shoved past me. She didn't get far. "I just saw him. That guy was drunk out of his mind and looking for a fight."

She held out her hand again, and Jason threw the keys to her. Without a word, she climbed into his black pickup truck and peeled out of the driveway while I stood there like a fool and watched. Jason didn't even care she was a wreck who was now behind the wheel and a threat to greater Los Angeles.

"Don't you ever want to be the overprotective brother?" I asked, all pissed off.

Jason shrugged. "Nope." He gave me our signature handshake, the same one we'd been doing for years.

"Fine. What did I miss?" I asked incredulously.

"The apocalypse." Jason headed back toward the house.

"Zombie apocalypse or cannibalistic aliens?" I joked.

"Just your run-of-the-mill nuclear war," Jason said. He stopped and looked at his house. The lights were all on and I could see Keith cleaning up the kitchen. "Want to get out of here?"

"Sure." It beat hanging around waiting for Lexi to come back tonight. Or not come back. "Ryan's party was lame. Want to grab some beers and go and see who's on the playground?"

Yeah, we still hung out on the playground. Except now, instead of climbing on the jungle gym, we drank beers on top of the tube slide. We'd only been there about an hour with some guys from our team when I got the text.

LEXI CELL: I need u.

I passed my Bud Light to Jason, jumped off the tube slide, and ran. No questions asked. I don't know how I knew where she'd be. I just assumed home. If she'd wrapped Jason's car around a tree somewhere, I doubt she could have texted me. I rolled up to the house for the third time that day and found her slumped up against the doorway, bleeding from the lip. Blood is on her tank top and white denim jacket. Then Whitney and Sam open the front door, both carrying duffel bags.

"Lexi!" Whitney cries and drops her bag. "What the hell happened?"

"Help me get her inside," I say, lifting her up. Lexi sways a bit as I try to help her stand. She smells like blood and beer. Whitney looks panicked, but she grabs Lexi's other arm and we half carry, half walk Lexi inside. Up the stairs, past the individual photos of the Connolly kids grinning like fools who didn't know what was going to soon hit them.

"I'll make coffee," Sam whispers since the only one not accounted for is Keith and we all assume he's asleep.

I don't ask how Sam knows how to make coffee either.

"It's not that bad," Lexi says as we get her into the bathroom. Whitney sits her on the ledge of the tub and Lexi almost falls off it.

"You're drunk and bleeding," Whitney says. "It's bad."

"Yeah, it's a little bad," Lexi slurs.

Whitney wets a washcloth and places it on Lexi's lip. She blots away the blood.

"If Jared hit you, I'll kill him," I say. "I really will."

"Me too," Whitney chimes in and we both look at her. "Not with my bare hands or anything, but we're learning archery in gym and I'm pretty good." Lexi tries to smile and winces.

Sam runs in with a mug that says: WORLD'S GREATEST MOM. I can smell the coffee. He passes the cup to Lexi and she takes a long sip. Sam yawns.

"Why don't you go to bed?" I suggest. "I can handle it from here."

"Are you sure?" Whitney asks, looking at Lexi.

She never stops worrying, that one. I lead her and Sam to the door. "I'm sure. I'll call you if I need you." Then I close the door behind me. Lexi sort of laughs as I kneel down beside the toilet and wash a drip of blood off her chin.

"Jared didn't hit me," Lexi says. I keep wiping away blood instead of saying anything. "It was so much worse than that. I walked in on him with another girl. I think her name was Sue Ellen."

I'm guessing it was the girl whose ass I saw him pinch. I

turn to the sink to wring out the washcloth. Blood washes down the drain.

"Who names their kid Sue Ellen unless they want her to be white trash?" Lexi asks.

I pull her hair back and wash the blood off her neck. Geez, you'd think she broke her jaw the way blood is just everywhere. I'm still not talking. I know I'll say something about Jared that will just set her off again.

"Anyway, she was doing, you know," Lexi says.

Yeah, I know.

"And I burst in screaming and she clocked me in the face," Lexi says. I see her eyes welling up. "Jared's cursing. Blood is going everywhere. People are running up to the bathroom and looking." She buries her face in her hands, wiping more blood on her shorts. "Oh God, everyone at the party saw us. They knew what he was doing in there with her. It was so humiliating."

Lexi slides off the tub and lies on the floor. Her lip is still bleeding like a river. Tears are falling down her face and she wipes them away before I can. Mascara and blood smear all over her cheeks. Her hair has blood in it too. She's a friggin' mess. I've got to get her cleaned up before Keith finds her. He'll never let her out of this house again.

I turn on the shower and let the steam fill the room. Lexi doesn't move. She's sobbing now. I take her hands and help her up again, but she falls into me. She's never going to be able to stand in the shower like this.

So I do what I have to do: I get in the shower with her.

I know, I know, big sacrifice on my part. It's not like I haven't thought about doing this with her a thousand times before. As I help her slip off her top and out of her shorts, and she's just standing there in a lace bra and panties, my body is aching to touch her. I want to run my hands all over her. But not right now. Not while she's bleeding and broken. Used and abused. Someone's got to put her back together first. Might as well be me.

I scrub the blood from her hands and her neck, feeling my shirt get damp and my arms grow cold from the spraying water. Lexi just stands there wordlessly and lets me clean her up. No wisecracks. No mouth. I hold back her hair while she lets the warm water run down her face and wash everything away. I wrap her in a towel after, then walk quietly down the hall to her room and find a pair of pajamas. She lets me put them on her. She even lets me walk her down the hall and put her into bed. I'm a little surprised when she pulls me into her bed with her, but I'm not going to argue. She pulls my arms around her waist, and the two of us just lie there in silence. We're thinking different things, I'm sure, as we wait for the dawn to give us a shot at another crappy day.

7 // WHITNEY

I was leaving, you know. Last night, when I found Lexi bleeding on the front doorstep, I was out of here. I couldn't sleep. What's new? I stared at my meds and spun the orange bottle around and around like a dreidel. I figured the spinning would work like hypnotism or something like that, but it didn't work.

I screwed over my family. I could see that now. Or I should say, I realized it when they all looked at me the way they did after dinner. Like I was a leper they wanted to avoid so they didn't break out in moron lesions too.

Why did I keep Dad's conversation with me from them? I don't know! At the time, I didn't think it was that big a deal. He was going for a ride to clear his head. That's what I told myself. When Lexi asked me where he was that night, I remember saying I don't know. Because I didn't. When Jason wanted to know why he wasn't making pancakes the next morning at breakfast, I covered for him and said he must have slept in. Dad needed space. I got that. I needed space a lot, which is why I spent so much of my nonsleeping time in my bedroom listening to Katy Perry and Pink songs.

But when Dad wasn't home by the following evening, and Lexi started to panic, Sam was crying, and Jason called Keith, I knew I had to commit to my lie for good. They were too wound up to understand all I saw Dad do was pull out of the car driveway. I didn't know he wasn't coming back. He didn't leave me a travel itinerary the way Mom always would when they went out of town. No, if I had said something when the world was crashing down around us, they would have killed me.

I should have known nothing would change six months later. If anything, now it's worse.

I just couldn't take the lie anymore. It was eating at me like a virus. Squeezing all other thoughts out of my mind.

"Now it's too late to do anything," I kept hearing Keith say over and over again in my mind.

Too late. Was it?

Those were the thoughts haunting me as I lay there in my dark room, the bright red glow from my digital clock making me feel like I was in Times Square. The numbers on my clock kept changing, but I was still wide awake. 11:55. 12:14. 12: 48. At 1:19, I finally turned on my Christmas lights and came up with an idea.

Maybe it wasn't too late to find Dad. Maybe I was the only one who knew where to look.

I was in my closet, throwing clothes in my red duffel bag, when Sam came up behind me, scaring the hell out of me. He was just standing there like a stalker in those Charlie Brown–looking pj's of his.

"What are you doing?" Sam asked. Jason jokes that I'm the fuzz, but Sam is even worse. He's the investigator. "Are you running away or something?" He yawned and I wondered if he was having trouble sleeping too.

Unlike Dad, I knew someone should know where I was going. "I'm going after Dad." Sam woke up quick when I said that. "I know I can find him."

"Are you insane?" Sam cried. "How are you going to go after him? On foot?"

I rolled my eyes. "No. I'm driving," I mumbled, and Sam raised an eyebrow. "Keith always leaves his car keys on the hall table."

Sam scratched his light brown hair. He was a tragic victim of bedhead. "But you don't know how to drive."

"I have a learner's permit," I said. Sure, no one had taken me out to practice driving since Dad left, but how hard could it be? I couldn't worry about parallel parking and three-point turns when there were more pressing things at stake. I needed to find Dad. "I can drive just fine."

Sam didn't say anything, and I wondered if he'd fallen asleep standing up. I walked to my dresser, grabbed two pairs of jeans, and when Sam wasn't looking, pulled out my babysitting money from its hiding place. I kept it stashed under the pillow on my dollhouse bed. I was pretty proud of myself for thinking of that spot. When I turned around again, Sam was still there. I wondered if he's going to argue with me. "Look, I'm going and there's nothing you can do to stop me."

For a moment, I saw a flash of fear in his eyes. Someone else is in his life was abandoning him too. I couldn't let him think that. I put my hands on his shoulders and stared into his oval-shaped brown eyes. "So are you coming with me or not?"

Sam slowly smiled. "Yeah, I'm coming."

I grinned. "Go pack." I stuck my money in the photo box and stuffed that in the duffel bag too. "And don't forget your toothbrush."

Sam looked confused. "Why?"

"Um, good hygiene?"

He nodded and I had the sneaking suspicion it had been a while since someone checked up on his brushing habits.

A few minutes later, we were sneaking down the stairs as quietly as possible. Every squeak sounded like an earthquake. Sam tripped and almost fell headfirst into his bicycle which was parked on the first staircase landing. I didn't want to stop and ask what it was even doing inside the house. I'd seen weirder things the last few months. Like the time I found Keith's kayak in the living room. We made it to the bottom of the stairs, grabbed Keith's keys from the hall table and a map of California that Dad always kept in the table drawer, and then tiptoed to the front door. With no appearance from a sleepy Keith or a just-getting-in Jason we were in the clear. I was just thinking about how Lexi probably wouldn't even come home, when I opened the front door and found her slumped on the steps like a rag doll, bleeding from her lip.

Zak was somehow running up the walkway to her rescue by the time I could blurt out, "Lexi? What the hell happened?"

Sam and I couldn't leave now. Not when Lexi was like this. If she or Zak spotted our bags, they didn't say anything. We all got to the business of putting Lexi back together—coffee, wet washcloths—only to have Zak suggest we both go to bed. I lingered for a moment till it got awkward and I felt a side effect of my meds coming on. I did not need to see Zak undress my sister and try to clean her up. I walked back to my room, imagining the two of them singing Pink's "Try." Two hours later, I was still wearing out my floor trying to decide what to do (Leave now? Leave tomorrow?). That's when Lexi stepped lightly into my room. Her hair was wet and she was wearing a fuzzy brown robe, but she looked a billion times better than she had just hours ago.

"Whit?" she said tentatively. "I'm sorry."

I just nodded.

She looked quickly at my duffel bag, still packed and ready, by my bed. "I'll go with you, okay?" she said. "To find him. I'll go with you tomorrow."

Lexi knew and she wasn't going to abandon me just like I wasn't going to abandon Sam.

"Okay," I said, exhaling slowly, the relief flooding through my veins. "We go tomorrow. Early. Before Keith gets up."

Lexi nodded and closed the door quietly behind her.

I didn't even need to set my alarm for the following morning. Who could sleep after everything that had happened that night and could happen tomorrow? Dad was out there and we were going to bring him home. I kept telling myself that over and over until I saw the sun peek through my window shades. When I crept out of my room and down the hall to wake Sam, Lexi was already in there getting him up. You couldn't even tell she had a busted lip the night before. The three of us tiptoed downstairs and began loading things in Jason's truck.

"Hurry," Lexi says as I shove Sam's blue bag in the trunk behind Lexi's zebra print one. "He's probably up already." I can't get the lift gate on the back of the truck to close. It keeps going back up and Lexi, so contrite last night, is growing impatient. "Hurry up!"

"Hurry up where?" we hear someone say.

It's Keith in a wifebeater and sweatpants, and Jason is right behind him wearing workout clothes for an early morning run.

Jason throws up his hands in disgust. "Great! We're all running away now?"

"We're going after Dad," I blurt out. No more lies. Keith and Jason just look at us. "We're going to follow the photographs in the box. I think he went to the places that made him happy when we were little. Places that would help him remember how great our family once was, you know?"

Jason nods slowly like he's in agreement, but Keith's jaw is set and I'm ready for him to come down on me. I pull my flannel shirt around me tight like armor. I'm not backing down on this. "You can come if you want, but we're going." I slam the back gate of the truck closed and walk around the side of the truck to get in. Sam does the same and Lexi heads to the driver's seat.

I'm so relieved I don't have to drive.

"Whoa!" Keith puts his hand on the driver's side door so Lexi can't get in. "No one's going anywhere."

We all start talking at once and I can't understand what anyone is saying. It's at that moment when I see Harry Freitas's black Lexus pull up.

"Great," Keith mumbles. "Just what we need. A party at seven a.m. Morning, Harry!" he says in a brighter tune.

Harry pulls on his navy sweater. He looks baffled to see us all outside. "Wow, you guys are up early."

"So are you," Keith says, crossing his arms over his chest. "What's going on?"

Harry looks from Sam in his oversize brown sweatshirt to Lexi in her short shorts and thick makeup and then at Keith. I hear a landscaper key up his mower in the distance. "Maybe we should talk alone."

For once, Keith looks at me. Really looks at me. "Whatever you have to say, you can say it to all of us. Secrets haven't been going so well in this family."

Harry sighs and runs a hand over his smooth, bald head. "Okay. Well, uh, last night there was a robbery at Mickey's Diner up on Route 27." He pauses and I wonder what he's getting at. "The police called me this morning. It seems the man matched your father's description and his car was the same make and model as your dad's as well."

I feel like the bottom has finally fallen out and we're about to be pulled into a sinkhole.

"Wait, wait, wait!" I can see Keith trying to process what Harry is telling us. "Let me get this straight. Our father has been missing for six months and *now* the police are accusing him of a local felony?"

Jason is bouncing up and down like he's ready for a boxing match. "No. No way. There's no way Dad would do that. Rob a diner? That's insane!"

Harry looks uncomfortable. "Yeah, well, I didn't think he'd skip out on his five kids either, but here we are."

Jason lunges at Harry so fast, he's just a blur. "Don't say that!"

Keith thankfully grabs Jason and pulls him back. "Hey, hey, he's just trying to help us," he says quietly.

Harry looks miserable. This man was my father's best man. He's Keith's godfather. He held Sam when he was born before my grandparents did. I know he's not out to get us. He just gets stuck with the sucky job of being the bad news bearer. "I'm sorry, Jason. I really am. I'm not telling you this to upset you guys. This all sounds crazy to me too." His eyes move from Jason to the rest of us. "The police just want to talk to you all and get a statement." He looks at a crack in our driveway. "They want to make sure he hasn't contacted you."

Jason huffs. I can tell he can't believe what he's hearing. I can't either. Dad would never rob a diner! He once made me bring a ChapStick back into a drugstore because they forgot to charge us for it. And why would he hang around so close to home and not come back to us? Something isn't adding up.

I can see Jason agrees with me. I watch as he comes and stands by the car. I see him put his hand on the passenger door handle. He's coming with us. I look hopefully at my older brother who's been sacked with so much responsibility. *Come help us find Dad*, I try to telepathically tell him. *You know he didn't do this.* Keith slowly nods and looks at Harry.

"If the police want a statement, tell them it will have to wait until Monday," Keith says. "We're going on a road trip." The rest of us try to contain our excitement.

"A road trip?" Harry asks, looking doubtful.

I don't blame him. We don't have two nickels to rub together, but this is it. Our last shot at finding Dad. Whether he's out there somewhere we remember or he was the one who robbed that diner, we'll forgive him. We just want him back.

"Yes, a road trip," Keith says, sounding more confident. He puts his arm around Sam and pulls him in close. I watch as Lexi and Jason hug each other. I never thought I'd see that happen again. Then I feel Jason's arm wind around me. Keith looks over and smiles at me. He doesn't say it, but maybe this means I'm forgiven. "We've been planning this road trip for a while," Keith tells Harry, his eyes on me. "It's a family thing."

Family. I've almost forgotten that's what we are. But as we head into the house to let Keith and Jason pack, I know for certain this trip is our chance to be one again.

8 // KEITH

Not ten minutes after I gruffly tell Harry our family is getting the hell out of Dodge, I feel like an ass and I'm on the phone apologizing to him.

Call it oldest child syndrome—I'm always taking knocks for things I have no control over. Mom dying, Dad disappearing, there being less than five thousand dollars left in our checking account—somehow these are the only matters people ask me about anymore. No one ever knows how to deal with our sucky issues, of course. They just look at me pathetically and ask how I'm doing.

Want to know how I'm doing? Shitty.

Who wouldn't feel shitty knowing they barely have enough money to keep the lights on even after selling Dad's vintage Porsche roadster that has sat covered in the garage for the last six months. But even that sale (that I had to beg Harry to let me make) isn't going to cover more than two *back* payments on our mortgage. We're almost a year behind apparently. Mortgage payments, sports and band signup fees, grocery shopping—how did this crap become the focus of my life?

I should be at UC San Diego, listening to a lecture on stem cell breakthroughs or dissecting a cadaver—something that both freaks me out and exhilarates me. Instead I'm here, playing Mom and Dad to my siblings and failing miserably at both.

"You hear what I'm saying, Keith?" Harry's voice is soft but firm with me. For a moment, I got so wrapped up in my own thoughts, I forgot he was on the line.

"Yeah, I hear you," I say. My godfather has as shitty a role in this mess as I do. Gone are the days Harry and I would talk about my latest girlfriend or my medical classes at UC San Diego. Hell, I don't even have the luxury of calling him Uncle Harry anymore. None of us do. When Dad left, it was like our relationship spun on its head and took on a whole new level. Now we talk about balancing bank accounts and getting access to Mom's will funds. Good times.

I stuff some T-shirts and underwear in the same back-pack I used in Ireland. I suspect this trip will be nowhere near as fun. "It's not like you're telling me anything new," I say to Harry, trying not to sound as agitated as I usually do when we have the same conversation over and over again. "I know we're broke. We shouldn't be going away with everything that's going on right now. But I told you—we're not going to spend much. We packed food. I already told everyone we're going to camp out at Emmet State Park." God, I hate how pathetic I sound.

"Wow, I haven't been to Emmet State Park since you kids were little." Harry sounds almost wistful. Then I hear him laugh and the sound surprises me. Normally Harry and my phone calls don't have laughter in them. "Your dad loved it at that campground so much there was a time when he wanted to try buy the place as an investment. Thankfully, I talked him out of it."

"Yeah, I'm not sure Mom was the campground owner wife type," I say with a grin. She always went along with us on camping trips, but there was no denying the fact she'd rather spend the weekend in Cabo San Lucas at a resort on a beach or visiting some gallery in Rome than camping in Southern California.

"Definitely not," Harry agrees and then he's silent for a moment. I continue to rummage through drawers for socks that match. "Have a good time." He hesitates. "I just want to be clear about this weekend, Keith. I know you're too smart for this, but as your family lawyer as well as your godfather, I should mention how much trouble you'd be in if you just took off with everyone and didn't come back."

I pause with a rolled-up pair of white socks in midair. "Harry, you know I'd never do that," I say, my jaw clenched. "What good would that do? We barely have enough money for a month's stay at a Motel 6." I feel myself getting angry again, and my fingers tighten around the pair of crew socks in my hand. "We'll be back tomorrow night. There's no escaping it."

There's no escaping this prison is what I really want to say.

That's what this house has become. A prison. I still replay the night Harry called me down in San Diego and told me that my father was missing. I half thought he was joking. Then when I realized he wasn't, I got angry. It was midsemester. I had a paper on in vitro fertilization due that Friday. "What do you want me to do about it?" I think I even said.

"Come home," I remember Harry telling me. "He's been gone a week. They've been staying with me for now, but Keith, if your dad doesn't show up soon, and you don't come home, I'll have to . . ."

I didn't like the way he hesitated. "You'll have to do what?" I asked.

"They're minors," Harry reminded me gently. "You're the only one of age. If you don't come back, I'll be forced to contact child protective services. They'll be placed in foster care."

I was home in hours. I don't even know how I got there or how fast I was driving. I'm not a total ass. My brothers and sisters were not getting split up and shipped out because my father had bailed and I was too into my own future to help them. I came home, called UC San Diego the next day to put my classes on hold, and I've been in this prison ever since.

There's that word again. Prison. As guilty as I feel for thinking that way, I know I'm not alone in these thoughts. We're all going through the motions every day—getting up, showering (Sam more reluctantly than the others), eating breakfast, going to school, or in my case, being pissed because I can't go to school, then coming home and hiding away from anything that reminds us of the life we lost. And the reminders are plenty. Like ghosts, Mom and Dad's pictures and mementos of our former life are everywhere in this palatial house, haunting us. There are days when I want to pack everything up in a box and stick it out in the garage. Then I catch Sam or Whitney holding a family photo lovingly while no one is watching and I abandon the plan.

When I think about it, my room is no different. It reminds me of a museum. Baseball trophies from high school still sit on shelves on the wall alongside ribbons from science competitions I've entered. A framed *Star Wars* lithograph I got for my sixteenth birthday is covered with dust alongside a photo collage my high school girlfriend Elise made me that I keep forgetting to take down. Maybe because I was never here long enough to care to do it. On college and medical school breaks, I always traveled, blowing into town for a long weekend or an occasional week and thinking of my old room like a hotel. I never thought I'd be back here permanently.

"Okay, I'm glad we understand each other." I hear the relief in Harry's voice. "Then try to have fun and good luck with everything. If you find anything or you need me, you can always call. Anytime, day or night."

"Thanks, I will," I manage to say, trying to remember Harry is only trying to help us—he's the *only* one trying to help us. I can't forget that. "Bye."

"Who was that?" Whitney stands in my doorway, her long, lanky frame leaning on the door. Her oval-shaped eyes seem to stare right through me like she knows my every fear and every thought. I wouldn't be surprised. Whitney is definitely the deep one in the family. I'm not sure if that's a good thing or it just means she's more tortured than the rest of us. "Was that the blonde from the other night on the phone?"

I smile to myself. She never misses a trick, this one. "No, the blonde broke up with me actually."

When Meghan showed up, I thought she was there to make me forget what my life had become. Turned out she was there to give me another reminder. I guess even girls in med school, who you'd think would be more mature than the rest of them at that stage, can't handle a long-distance relationship, especially when that long-distance relationship is with a guy who might eventually become permanent guardian to four brothers and sisters. Having a boyfriend with an insta-family is a real mood crusher apparently. Fifteen minutes after we busted in on Whitney screaming in her room, Meghan's tail lights in the distance were the only thing left of her.

Just another winning moment in the current life of Keith Connolly. At least I was smart enough to keep my bitter thoughts to myself. I had to put on a show for the rest of them. "The blonde and I had been over for a while anyway," I lie to Whitney. "You know I can't be with a girl who doesn't like *Star Wars*."

Whitney's thick eyebrows, that someday could make her a model if she ever grows comfortable in her own skin, rise slightly. "Absolutely not! Any girl who doesn't like the Jedi Order can't be trusted." We smile at each other for a moment, our normal relationship back if just for a brief blip in time. "I'm sorry, though."

And we're back.

"If it helps, I'm sure she was probably a sociopath." Whitney plays with the crystal doorknob, letting it rotate and I look at her. She's not joking. "Ten percent of the population is, you know."

I shake my head. "Where do you learn this stuff?"

"My shrink," she says as if it should be obvious.

I'm the one who sent her to him. I may be sucking big-time in every other area of my family's lives, but when it comes to emotions, I spotted Whitney's meltdown right away. I'm no medical genius, but anyone could see all her crying, outbursts, and panicky thoughts weren't just grief. She needed a way to cope. We all do. We just don't all need pills to do it. But maybe I'm wrong about that. I have no clue what's going on with Jason and Sam, and Lexi is becoming a total slut. If I catch that guy Jared here again, I'm worried I'll be arrested for busting his lip open.

"So who was really on the phone?" Whitney presses again, a smile playing on her lips.

She'll make a good lawyer or private eye someday. "Emmet State Park," I lie again. Lying has become so natural that half the time I don't realize I'm doing it. "I wanted to reserve a camping spot for tonight." Whitney looks satisfied with that answer. "You should finish packing so we can get going. Tell the others we're leaving in twenty minutes." I zip up my bag. "And tell Sam to find the lanterns. Jason is looking for our pop-up tent. I think both are in the garage."

Whitney nods. "Anyone else call? I heard the phone ring twice."

God, I can't fool her and I know she's not going to go away until I throw her a bone. "Oh, Zak's parents called too." At least this time I'm telling the truth. "They're going on a weekend getaway to try to save their marriage. Again. And since the last time they left Zak alone—"

"He threw a party with Jason and almost burned down their house?" Whitney finishes.

"Good memory," I say. "They don't want a repeat of that scenario so he's coming with us. You don't care, do you?"

"*I* don't," she says and there is a hint of something I can't put my finger on in her voice. I ignore it. There's only so many girl emotions I can handle deciphering in any given day—Lexi's are enough to blow the system—and it's only 9:00 a.m.

"Good." I pull the sheets up on my bed and try to make it presentable. For who, I don't know. It's not like Meghan is coming back. "I don't care either. Zak's here almost as much as we are anyway. And I could care less who joins us as long as we all get out of here for a while."

"Yeah, me too," Whitney agrees. She picks up my bag and begins walking out of the room. "You're not the only one who's ready to leave this town in the dust."

My stomach clenches tightly. I guess I'm fooling no one, even though I keep my thoughts to myself 90 percent of the time. "Yeah, it will be good to get away for a bit," I agree and Whitney partially closes the door behind her.

Alone again, I look around to make sure I haven't forgotten anything. I'm sure I'm missing something. I'm no Mom, so I go through my checklist again and realize I don't have Dad's travel must-have on me: a AAA card in case we break down and need to get towed (hey, with this family's shitty luck, that's a real possibility).

I open my desk drawer to look for it and instead see my passport staring back at me. The blue vinyl book seems to be there solely to taunt me, but I can't resist pulling it out anyway. I sit down on my bed and torture myself as I flip through the pages. I've collected a nice group of stamps since high school. Dad and I spent two weeks exploring Australia as my high school graduation gift (who needs a lame party when you can snorkel in the Great Barrier Reef?). In college, I took my first summer off to go to Dublin with my roommate, Liam, and we spent three weeks touring landmarks and pubs I barely remember after drinking so many pints of Guinness.

Then there was that amazing semester abroad in England junior year when I almost switched to a science major. I nearly gave Mom a heart attack because she said she always knew I was meant to be a doctor. At parties, she would talk about the time Whitney slipped on a wet stoop in flip-flops and shattered her ankle in three places. I kept her—and the twins who freaked out when they saw the bone poking through—calm till the ambulance got there. I even wrapped Whitney's ankle to keep it stable till Mom could get home from wherever she was at.

But that wasn't what hooked me on medicine. I owe that to Sam. The day he was born, more specifically. When Dad brought us all in to see Sam after Mom gave birth, I was into it, but let's be honest, I'd done this dance three times before.

So there I was, hanging out in the room, pretending to ooh and aah over Sam the way Lexi and Whitney were, when what I was really doing was hanging back by the door so I could witness the action going on across the hallway. A woman went into labor so quickly they could barely get her into the stirrups in time let alone close the curtain in the room. I watched the whole thing. My guy friends have a ton of jokes about this crucial career moment, and how it made me want to be an ob-gyn. I get it. Hell, I've made the jokes myself, but the truth is, nothing seemed cooler to me than helping bring a life into this world. It kills me to think I'm not going to be doing that. Sure, I could transfer somewhere closer, but how would I have time for classes, papers, residency—let alone studying—when I'm raising four kids?

I stare at an empty page in my passport. The page that should have a stamp that says Brazil on it. I was going to spend my summer off before medical school there, working as a volunteer in a medical facility and giving pregnant women care. But then Mom got sick, and all any of us wanted to do was be home with her.

Now I can't wait to ditch this house even if it's just for the weekend.

Dad, where the hell are you?

How could you screw up all of our lives and make me pick

up the pieces? Don't you realize I have a life of my own to live? I'm supposed to be a doctor. Not picking up your leftovers.

I sigh heavily and run a hand through my hair. I look in the streaky mirror that could use Windex and stare at my reflection grimly. I can't believe I just called my family "leftovers."

Maybe Whitney isn't the one who needs medication after all.

"I found the tent!" I hear Jason yell upstairs.

Sounds of arguing in the kitchen follow. The voices sound like Lexi and Zak. The two of them are always at each other's throats lately. Sexual tension if I've ever seen it, not that I want to think of Lexi sleeping with someone. I already want to pummel Jared's face. God knows those two aren't spending innocent nights at the ArcLight movie theater.

"Great!" I try to sound enthusiastic. Excited. Anything but what I really am, which is desperate. Desperate for Dad to return, for me to get my life back, for my brothers and sisters not to be so wounded, and for this nightmare to disappear. "Put it in the truck. I'll be down in a minute. Tell everyone to finish up—and don't forget your toothbrushes!" I hear Sam groan. "They're mandatory!"

"You got it, boss," Jason says. "And I'm calling it right now— I've got shotgun!"

Sam groans loudly again. "I want shotgun on the trip back!"

"Deal," I hear Jason say as Lexi and Zak's arguing grows to a fever pitch.

"Let's get out of here," Whitney tries to move everyone along. "If we leave now, I won't challenge either of you to a shotgun duel all weekend."

"Good," Jason says, "because you'd lose. You run like a girl."

Whitney snorts. "I do not!" I hear her hit him and then the door slam. Even Zak and Lexi have stopped fighting. The house is quiet again and I feel myself relax.

For once, my brothers and sisters don't sound ticked off with me. And I'm not acting like the parent I'm not. I'm just their older brother, which is how it should be.

9 // WHITNEY

I almost forgot my cell phone! I run back upstairs to my room and find it plugged into the wall socket exactly where I left it. I pull the charger out and turn the phone on. I know there's something else I'm forgetting to do, but for the life of me, I can't remember what it is. I head back into the hallway, almost tripping on a lone blue baseball sock that's lying on the floor next to a baseball mitt outside Jason's door that has sat there all week. Someone seriously has to start cleaning up around here. Not only is it disgusting, but the stench from Sam and Jason's rooms, which probably have dirty laundry in it from 2013, is unbearable. Sometimes when they leave for school before me, I sneak in there with Glade Hawaiian Breeze air freshener and give it a quick spray.

When I pass by Keith's room again, the door is ajar, and I can see him in there, just staring at his passport like he wants to cut and run. When I see him when no one's watching, he looks like he needs the meds more than I do. Sitting on the edge of his unmade bed in jeans and a gray button-down shirt, he's lost in his own thoughts and I sense they're dark ones. How many more days do we have in this house if we don't find Dad? Would a judge even award Keith permanent custody of Jason, Lexi, Sam, and me when he's years away from having a career as a doctor? What will he do if we cost him the chance to become one? Will he have to go work at the Gap, like the She-Bitches keep saying to me?

The thoughts make me remember it's time for my meds. I pull the container out of my pocket and swallow the pill without water. Take one enough times and you become a master at swallowing pills in any situation. I wait for the pill to go into effect. Sometimes it does right away, other times it could take an hour. All I know is I'll need it to work for this car trip I've dragged everybody into. I've gotten them psyched to find Dad. What if every place we stop is a dead end?

I hear banging and look through the door again at Keith. He's tapping his legs and stomping his feet as he sits on the bed, his movements making a familiar sound that reminds me of the song "Cups" sung by Anna Kendrick. In my head, Keith is surrounded by a haze as he rises and starts to sing the words I've said to myself so many times before. I hope he's not going anywhere but on this trip with us. I slide out of the way and press my body against the wall as Keith leaves the room without seeing me. He's singing louder now, tapping the stair railing as he descends the stairs, jumping off the final landing and dancing into the living room like he's performing onstage in *Pitch Perfect*. I like thinking of Keith that way. Happy to get out of town with us.

I know I'm up for ditching this town for the weekend. I just wish I could remember what I have to do before I go!

Homework? It's a Saturday so there is none.

Toothbrush? I have mine and Sam's since I'm the only one who seems to care about hygiene.

Map? Portable GPS? I've got both. Lexi said the GPS was already in the car. Dad lived for that device. He needed it being a Realtor. The GPS helped him fake out clients. He always claimed to know exactly where to go when he was really just plugging an address into the device.

Flashlights for camping. That's it! I forgot to tell Jason to find the flashlights in the hall closet. I open my bedroom door and jump back.

"Ready?" Susan asks cheerily. My best friend is wearing our red-and-white band uniform cap that makes us look like horse jockeys. She frowns and adjusts her lavender frames that bounce off the light in my room and reflect back my outfit—a flannel shirt and jeans. "Where's your white tee you're supposed to wear for the car wash? Did Keith forget to do the laundry again? Well, you can't wear that white tee you wore to the pep rally. I told you it would take at least a week to get that rotten egg stench out of your clothes." She shakes her head, her blonde curls whipping around her face like a necklace. "You've got to hand it to the She-Bitches. Who else would be clever enough to throw expired eggs at us? Cruel but clever." Her brown eyes widen. "God, I hope they don't bring eggs to the car wash today." She shudders. "They wouldn't, would they? The whole football team will be there!"

I slap my head. "The band car wash! I completely forgot!" I bite my lip. "I can't go."

"What?" Susan shrieks. "Why?" She doesn't give me time to answer. "You have to go! We're raising money to go to the state competitions and I can't go alone." She grips my shirt and pulls me toward her, practically pulling me out of my room. Jason walks by with camping tent poles and looks at us strangely. "Please don't ditch me, Whit. The She-Bitches are going to hang out at the car wash all day to make fun of us."

I adjust the helmet's strap around Susan's chin. "You'll be fine," I say soothingly and realize I sound a lot like Mom when she was forcing me to try out for the Color Guard and I didn't want to. "I have a family emergency, so I can't go." Susan makes a small gurgling sound and for a moment I fear she's choking. I wave my hand nonchalantly and try to seem unconcerned. "But you don't need me there."

"Need you there?" Susan repeats. "Of course I need you there! Last year they tried to drown us in our own buckets. In fact, I'm pretty sure the only reason we're still alive is that it's harder to bury two bodies instead of one."

"I found the camping lanterns!" Sam yells upstairs. Susan and I back up and look over the railing where my brother is holding two battery-operated lights. "Anyone find the sleeping bags yet?"

"I think they're in the attic above the garage." I hear Lexi say, her voice traveling from downstairs. "I'll go look for them."

"Wait, you guys are going camping?" Susan asks.

At that moment, my cell phone rings in my hands. The screen says: NO CALLER ID.

Susan and I look at each other. "The She-Bitches," we both huff and then sigh.

Their MO is to keep calling till they get you. Sometimes they keep calling even *after* they've reached you. I've found it's better to just get the humiliation over with quickly so they hopefully get bored. Instead of hemming and hawing, I pick up on the first ring and put the call on speaker so Susan can hear my torture firsthand.

"Hello?" I say, finding my voice. I try to sound calm, collected and not at all concerned, which is the exact opposite of how I feel every time they call.

"Rise and shine, Whit!" I hear one of their voices sing. The sound makes me think of acid. "Time for your little car wash to raise money for the band geek trip."

In the background we hear the "awwws."

"We'll be there to egg you on," the girl says. "Get it?" They all burst out laughing. "See you there. I'm sure you'll be coming alone. With Lexi getting beat up last night after getting it on with Jared in that bathroom, I'm sure she's way too hung over to help you!" *Click.*

"Why am I bringing this phone with me again?" I ask Susan.

"We've got to find a way to get rid of them," Susan agrees. "Don't make me face them alone today." She reaches for my hand and squeezes.

I squeeze back. "I know, I'm sorry. This trip just happened so quickly." I fill her in fast on the conversation with Harry and the fight that broke out last night at dinner. "We're going after my dad."

"Wait, you told them everything?" Susan asks as Jason runs by with pillows.

I nod. "It was a disaster, then it went better, but it was still a disaster. But now we're going after him together. We're going to track him down." I put my arm around her. "You understand, right?"

"We leave in ten minutes!" I hear Keith say from down the hall.

Susan hugs me. "Damn you and your good excuses. I'll see you on Monday—if I'm not mortally wounded." She heads to the staircase.

"If you are, I promise to avenge your death," I tell her, following her down the stairs. She gives a little wave on her way out the door. I wave back, then turn around and bang into Sam.

"Are you sure our first stop on this trip down memory lane is a good idea?" he asks and I follow him into the kitchen. Lexi comes up behind us and places a cooler and sweatshirts on the kitchen island. She's dressed in a loose black skull tank top, gray skinny jeans, and her white denim jacket. The blood stains are gone, so I guess someone finally did a load of wash around here.

"He'll be fine," I say, thinking of Jason who walks by at that moment with a large bag of Cool Ranch Doritos. "But if we fail there, where to after Emmet State Park?"

Sam pulls a photograph out of his pocket and shows it to us. In the picture, we're a few years younger and we're wearing knights helmets and carrying swords. "Castle Park," Sam reminds us.

Lexi takes the picture from him and looks at it closely. A smile plays on her lips. "You had your birthday party there one summer, Sam, remember?"

"Best birthday party ever," Sam says, a far-off look in his eyes. The ice machine in the fridge kicks on, and I hear the tiny *clink* of cubes hitting the tray.

"I think Dad liked it there even more than you did," Lexi adds and moves toward the fridge to get a drink. She grabs a glass from the nearest cabinet and fills a cup with crushed ice. It's hard to hear her over the machine. "He never missed a chance to watch a jousting match." She wrinkles her nose. "No matter how bad those horses smelled in the heat."

Sam and I lock eyes. I give the photo back to him. "Smelly horses or not, it's a good idea to go there."

I hear the front door open and get quiet, worrying Jason is back to ask where we're off to first. Instead, I see Zak in a hoodie, carrying a backpack and a sleeping bag with him. My stomach tightens when I see Lexi's face.

She does a double take. "You're coming with us?"

Zak grins so wide, I'm afraid his cheeks might crack. He leans his arms on one of the bar stools and stares only at Lexi. "Yep. I figured you can't survive without me." She rolls her eyes.

I never understood why Lexi gives Zak such a hard time. Even if you took away his baseball god status, Zak would rank as one of the most popular guys at University High. He looks like a *GQ* model with his wavy, longish dirty-blond hair, and has the body of one too, but his personality is even better in my book. It would be easy for Zak's ranking to keep him from talking to band geeks like Susan and me, but he's genuinely decent to people in our school no matter what their social ranking or sports standing. No matter how rough of a time he gives Lexi, I know he's got her back.

"Besides, someone's got to keep an eye on you," Zak adds, walking up to Lexi and thrusting his sleeping bag into her arms.

"You can't be left alone. You're a danger to yourself."

Maybe I gave him too much credit.

Lexi shoves the sleeping bag back into his arms and looks up at him. "I'm a WHAT?"

Clink! Another few cubes of ice drop into the tray in the machine. Sam exhales slowly and I bite my lip. Zak really knows how to get her going.

"Danger to yourself," he repeats in case she was the least bit confused, which of course she wasn't. Lexi gets in his face and lets the sleeping bag drop to the ground. Zak holds up his hands to surrender. "Hey, I'm not the one who drank too much last night so they could forget they were dating a cheating asshole."

Ouch! That was very She-Bitch-like of him to say and I don't think I'm the only one who thinks that. Lexi just stands there, one of her hands gripping the bottom of her tank top, the other hand pawing at her jeans. Her black nail polish is so glossy, it rivals the sheen on the stainless-steel appliances. Now that I look a little closer at our stove, I realize it might not be that shiny anymore.

"Child present," Sam jokes, trying to lighten the mood. He jumps up on the island, his dirty sneakers hitting the cabinets. If Keith were in here, he'd freak out, but Lexi and Zak ignore him. What else is new?

"Screw you, Zak," Lexi stumbles over her words. "Sometimes

you can be such a great guy," she says softly and I see Zak raise an eyebrow. "And other times you can be so . . . you can be so . . ."

Zak folds his arms and leans back against the island. He grabs a bright green apple from the bowl and takes a bite. "Honest? Helpful? Charming?"

"A douche!" Lexi declares, moving toward him instead of away. They're standing so close now they're practically slow dancing. Sam and I watch the moment unfold like it's from one of those mushy love movies Jason always makes fun of me for watching. "At least I went for it with someone. That's more than I can say about you."

Sam leans over to me and whispers in my ear. "They like each other, right?"

"Shh," I say, leaning farther back as Lexi's arms start flying. The two of them are trading barbs faster now. "They're the only ones who don't seem to know that yet."

"Jared called me and apologized." I hear Lexi say and realize maybe Sam and my love radar might be off a tick. She pulls her long, wavy dark hair away from her face. "Things are all good between us."

Zak drops the apple he's eating in the garbage with a look of disgust. "You're kidding right? You're going back to a guy who cheated on you? God, you're so stupid." His voice rumbles and my heart rate races. The room takes on a blue tint and I know my hallucinations are about to take over again.

Lexi looks like she's been smacked. She begins backing out of the kitchen slowly like she's too dangerous to stay in the same room as him. She pulls a wooden spoon from a canister of kitchen utensils and points it in Zak's direction. "Stay away from me."

Zak throws up his hands. "We'll be in the same car all weekend. Good luck with that one!"

Lexi disappears down the hall and I feel like she has a rainbow of colors following her. "I'm good at pretending you're not here, so I'm sure it won't be a problem."

"Guys, we should get going." I hear Keith call from the front door. I see him set the house alarm. "Everyone out." Sam and I look at each other before he jumps off the island and follows Keith out the front door.

When we reach the car, I can see the back is completely full with camping gear. Jason is already in the front passenger seat, staring out the window. He taps the window with his finger absentmindedly and it makes a small pinging sound. Zak squeezes his bag into the back as Lexi jumps in the car without even a glance in his direction. She makes her way to the back of the car and pops a piece of gum in her mouth, chewing angrily as Zak climbs in after her. Thankfully for all of us, he takes one of the captain's seats in the second row. Sam takes the seat next to him and I climb in the back. A cooler sits between Lexi and me. I try to make eye contact with my sister, but she's clearly not in the mood to talk right now. I watch her dark lips blow a bubble with her gum and let it pop, then blow another one. One row ahead of me, I see Sam stick his finger in his mouth and make a popping sound while Zak appears to be tapping his thigh to an unknown beat. When Keith gets in the front seat and I hear the engine roar to life sounding like a song, I know these sounds must all be in my head. We're not really singing "Cups," although, I half wonder if I asked Jason to turn on the radio and the song was on, if everyone wouldn't sing along. We all seem to have our own reasons to want to get out of town this weekend.

As we pull out of the driveway and begin to cruise down our block, the bushes whirring past us, joggers flying by in their expensive workout gear and nannies wheeling kids in strollers, I know I'm not going to miss being gone for the weekend. My cell phone is with me, but off so I can't hear from Susan (forgive me, bestie) about how horrible the car wash is or watch the NO CALLER ID call come up on my phone again. I don't want to talk to the She-Bitches. This weekend is about finding Dad.

Jason's tapping gets louder, Lexi's bubbles sound more frequent, and Keith revs the engine as we turn the corner and approach a long, smooth straightaway. Sam pulls out the map we've outlined in red to try to retrace steps Dad might have taken when he tore out of our driveway six months ago and never looked back. *Please let us find him and bring him back home,* I think. *I know we can convince him to come back. I don't care what's happened, I just want him to come back.*

Soon I see the familiar green sign that says Route 684/Runyon Canyon. We've passed it a zillion times before, but this time, it takes on new meaning. I watch as my brothers and sisters all turn their heads and stare at the words that lie below it: YOU ARE NOW LEAVING SAN BERNARDINO COUNTY. WE HOPE YOU ENJOYED YOUR VISIT! For once, I know we're all thinking the same thing—when we're gone, you're going to miss us when we're gone.

10 // JASON

Have you ever been to a baseball game? Like a *real* baseball game?

I'm not talking about your brother's shitty T-ball game or even college ball. I'm talking the Major Leagues. Think the Dodgers versus the Giants. My dad used to take me to watch them all the time. I'm a pitcher, so you're probably thinking I spend all nine innings with my eyes locked on the pitcher on the mound.

I'm not.

Know what I focus on? The guys on the rival team's bench. And their coaches. I watch like a hawk. The other team wants to get inside a pitcher's head, figure out what makes him tick, what he's going to throw and when he's getting tired. The trick is to fool them all. "You see the way they're watching the catcher's signals, Jay?" my dad would ask me. He's the one who taught me to watch the other team's dugout for signs. "They're sure he's going to throw a curveball next, but if he's smart, he's going to fake them out and go with a slider or a changeup." My dad looked at me sharply. "Never show them all your cards, kid. Keep them guessing."

That's what I've gotten good at, on and off the field: keeping people guessing.

I guess my old man was pretty good at that move himself. None of us have a clue why he left. This road trip Whitney cooked up is supposed to help us figure it out. I don't want to be a total shit, especially when Sam seems particularly chipper for a change, but I don't think Dad left a trail of clues behind like breadcrumbs. He's not a guinea pig. We can't lure him out on a trip down memory lane. People who don't want to be found aren't.

I feel someone shake me and I open my eyes.

"Everyone up." I hear Keith say. "We're at our first stop."

I pretend to stretch and yawn like I've been asleep the whole time. Really I just had my eyes closed so I wouldn't have to make small talk. It's not like I'm going to miss much. Lexi's griping, Sam's cheering, and the family SUV is coming to a stop. I roll my neck around. I can hear the cracks as I move my head, which feels tight from leaning against the car window for an hour or was it two? Where are we anyway? I stare down at the GPS, but it's just a map with a lot of words and green and blue grids that mean nothing to me. I quickly wipe the drool that's dribbled from my mouth onto the glass before anyone notices. I guess that's what I get for daydreaming about ball. Nice.

I yawn again—loudly—and Lexi gives me a disgusted look. She's one to talk about being disgusting. I'm about to say something about hanging out with a scumbag like Jared Reinhart when I finally look out the window. The view is familiar and I'm trying to figure out why as I open the passenger door and climb out of the truck. Where are we? A park? In front of me there's a huge stretch of beaten-down grass and a bike path where riders and early morning joggers are pounding the pavement. We're not at the campground, that's for sure. No one's even walking around. My family is lined up next to the car like they're greeting a royal or some crap like that and I'm confused as to why. Zak shrugs, like he doesn't get it either. Then I get a look at Whitney. You can always tell what's going on by looking at her and right now she's fidgeting worse than she does when I see her at her locker at school. Whitney's locker is next to that Kardashian wannabe, Melanie whatsherface. I have no idea if those two are friends. I tune out the high school hallway bullshit. Nothing sobers a person up quicker than going from a fat wallet life to almost an orphan in less than a year.

Now I keep them guessing. I keep my head down, my mouth shut, and go through the motions when I'm anywhere but home and chilling with Zak. I got called in to the school psychologist's last month. I never told Keith that. I never told anyone that. Not even Zak. I may not be playing the way I once was, and maybe I'm too tired to bother to raise my hand in class (and who would want to when we're taking about carbon and its compounds and the U.S. Constitution and shit?), but I'm not *loco*. I don't think Whit is nuts either, but who am I to tell her whether she needs meds?

Clink! The familiar sound of metal hitting a ball makes me spin around. "What the . . . ?" On the opposite side of the car is a ball field, but I realize quickly not just any one.

Whitney leaves the lineup and comes up to me with a panicked look on her face. "Don't freak out."

The dugouts, the stands, the small snack stand, and electronic scoreboard. This is no crappy local school field. Take one look at the local ads on the side fence for Antonio's AUTHENTIC NEW YORK SLICES OF PIZZA IN SO. CAL and Taste of Home Realty or the video booth and you know this place is several steps up from that. In the distance, I notice a guy Dad's age watching us. He throws his ball bag into the back of his car and walks toward us.

Sam hands Whitney the wooden box that holds the family photos and Whitney pulls out one on top. I recognize it right away. I'm wearing a royal blue Dodgers uniform on the pitcher's mound and Dad snapped a photo of me winding up to throw a screwball.

"It was one of the photographs Dad was looking at the night

he left," she says guiltily. Lexi watches my reaction closely, but says nothing.

I rip the picture from Whitney's hand and stare at it closely. The concentration on my face, the sweat on my brow, the fierce determination running through my veins . . . I don't know who that is anymore. "You sabotaged me!" I say and let the picture flutter to the ground, the wind picking it up for a moment before sending it sailing into the dirt. Dust plumes up around the photo and Whitney hands Lexi the photo box so she can dive for the picture. She dusts it off on the leg of her jeans.

"Um, what's going on?" Zak asks, looking from me to Lexi who responds by turning her back toward him.

Keith walks around the car to get closer to the field. "This is where Jason pitched his first no-hitter." He looks at me as if he's trying to jog my memory. "This is where you had your Little League championship game."

Lexi stands next to Keith and faces the field. She snaps a bubble. "And Dad went, like, ballistic he was so proud, remember?"

"So it is you!" I hear the guy say and I realize he's talking to me. I stare into his gray eyes, and see the deep lines on his face that spread out like a grid. He adjusts his white-and-blue cap and the image comes flooding back to me. I've seen this guy do that move a thousand times, but I'm not ready to admit that. "You're Jason Connolly, right?" he says, beating me to the punch. He scratches the stubble on his chin. He's wearing a San Marino Blue Jays logo on his maroon shirt. He turns sideways and I catch a glimpse of the back. Double digits and the name Sullivan decorate it. "You had a killer curveball at ten years old!"

The look Keith gives me, along with a pat on the back, is classic Dad. "That's him," he says, sounding proud. The thought makes me want to hurl. And I had a big bowl of Lucky Charms before I left.

Keith is nowhere close to being Dad. Not today. Not ever. And I hate it when he tries to play the part. I stare angrily at the tops of my dirty black Converse sticking out from the bottom of my jeans.

"Pat Sullivan," the coach says, shaking Keith's hand.

"Keith Connolly," my brother tells him. "And these are our sisters, brother and, uh, family friend."

"What's up?" Zak says, and shakes the coach's hand. "Great ball field you got there."

We all look at the field. For real grass, it's in pretty good shape. The painted lines outlining the boundaries are brighter than my white T-shirt (I guess it would help if someone taught me how to use bleach), and there's not a piece of trash or gum anywhere the eye can see. They've kept this place nice. I watch as a father and son walk on to the field with a bat and ball. The kid can't be more than nine or ten and he has the same annoyingly curly brown hair I had at his age. The difference between us is he's wearing a Giants cap and I'm a Dodgers guy all the way. They talk intently for a minute, discussing strategy like my dad always did with Zak and me, and the boy goes to home plate to wait. The kid is nearly bouncing out of his skin as he lifts the bat and prepares to take his dad's first pitch. *Clink!* He hits a line drive on the first swing. Not bad.

I watch the father run over and high-five him, then pulls his son's cap off and rubs the kid's head. The boy's laugh bounces off the dugouts and pierces my eardrum. I exhale slowly and turn away.

Better enjoy that family batting practice while you can, kid.

Coach Sullivan stares at the ballpark and the kid playing proudly, his thick black eyebrows creased intently. "It is nice, isn't it? They're putting in state-of-the-art lights so we can play at night at the end of this season, and rumor is we might even switch to turf if we get one more winning Little League championship here." He turns back to me. "So? What about you? I heard your high school team ranked nationally last year. Are you looking to play college ball?"

And there it is. The elephant in the room. The question I've managed to avoid among friends, the weary school guidance counselor, and even with my ball coach.

"You're going to have to pick a school soon," I can hear my coach saying in that deep Irish brogue of his. How the guy wound up being a baseball coach in Southern California is beyond me. He says he sucked at rugby in Dublin as a kid and had to find something else to do with his time. "The scouts are going to be coming out in droves to see you play this season, Connolly. I want you ready."

I wasn't. After all that crap with my parents, and Keith coming home and pretending to be all authoritative, throwing a mean fast ball seemed stupid. Who cared how fast my arm was when we're worried about keeping the freaking lights on? Yeah, I'd seen the past due bills. Just because Keith tried to hide them in Dad's old office didn't mean they didn't exist. When he first got back he tried to come to some of my games. The others too, but I could see them in the stands. Keith all distracted and on his phone 90 percent of the time. Whitney worried about who was sitting around her. Lexi focused on Zak and pretended not to be. I don't even know what Sam was doing. Half the time, none of them would know the game's stats afterward even if I had a good game. At least Zak's parents, as shitty as they are, were there for my no-hitter. Not Keith. It finally got to the point when I just stopped telling them when games were. When Dad was still around, he tried to make it to some of my games too, but you could tell he was distracted. Sometimes he'd leave halfway through the game. After Dad had been gone for a few weeks, and my siblings forgot I even played a sport, I stopped showing up to practice. Coach chewed me a new one a couple of times, but I've gotten good at tuning people out. I sure as hell don't want anyone coming to see me now.

I scuff the ground with my sneaker and watch the dust get picked up by the wind and move it around. "Yeah, I don't think college ball is in the cards for me anymore."

"Wait, what?" Keith looks like he might rupture a blood vessel in his face. The blue vein that pops along his forehead, just like Dad's used to, is sticking out.

"I'm over it, okay?" I go from zero to angry in under five seconds when I see Keith's reaction. Who's he to judge? He's not even in school right now. "It's just not my thing anymore." I hear another *clink* of a ball and don't have it in me to turn and see how far the kid hit the ball this time. "It was always Dad's obsession, not mine."

"What are you talking about? You love baseball!" Keith says, but I ignore him. It's easier to just pull my earphones out of my pocket, stick them in my ears, and go stand at the other end of the car away from their judging eyes. I hit my music app and pretend to play a new Passenger song. Childish, I know. What can I say? I don't want to talk, but I kind of want to hear what Keith and this guy are going to say about me.

"Zak, spill it." I hear Lexi say instead.

"No way." Zak's no dumb-ass. I pretend to be nodding my head to the music while Zak backs away from Keith like he's about to burst into flames. "I'm staying out of this. It's none of my business."

Keith's one step ahead of him. Literally. He puts his hand firmly on Zak's shoulder, pulling his gray T-shirt in his hands. "Not your business? You practically live with us, so I'm thinking you fall under the same Connolly code as we all do." He motions to Lexi, Sam, and Whitney. "Tell me what's up. Now. Or I will get you a bus ticket to San Diego where your parents are staying for the weekend."

Shit. He's got Zak there. I see Zak sigh and know he's going to give me up. It's not like it's any big secret. Most of University High could tell Keith the same story.

Zak's brown eyes dart back and forth at lightning speed, just like I've seen them do when he's at second base trying to decide how risky it would be to steal home (usually not very risky, he's the top base stealer on the team). "Jason hasn't been able to strike anyone out since your dad left. . . . Hell, he can't even throw a decent curveball anymore."

"Why didn't you tell us?" Keith raises his voice, then remembers the coach is standing there hearing this whole thing. He tries to smile. "How could you keep this a secret?"

"Because we should have noticed, okay?" Sam shouts, startling even me who's supposed to be listening to loud music. "You don't even take us to his games anymore!"

Lexi's jaw drops slightly and her gum falls out of her mouth and onto the coach's shoe. Whitney's cheeks flush and she bends down to pick the gum up in a piece of wrapper.

Sam turns to look at the rest of us, me included. "I mean, right now, you all kinda suck big time. I'm sick of this pathetic, loser, self-absorbed crap!" I'm so surprised I actually pull my earphones out of my ear. "If Mom and Dad were here, they'd be super pissed at all of you."

Lexi snorts. "And not you?"

Sam turns on her. "Nope. I'm the only one still normal around here. It's just no one has the time to notice!" He starts to storm off then turns back to Lexi again. He rips the photograph box she's been holding out of her hands. "And you're wearing too much eye makeup!"

We all stand there, dumbfounded, even the coach, and watch Sam run into the park. Lexi's cheeks are bright pink as she tears off in the opposite direction. No shocker here. Seconds later, Zak follows her like a lovesick puppy. I keep telling him to play it cool, but he doesn't.

"I'll go after him." I hear Whitney say. She runs past and I notice the picture of me at the Little League game fall on the ground.

Keith glances my way, and I quickly put on some music for real this time. "Safe and Sound" by Capital Cities fills my earphones. I close my eyes and try to listen.

My instinct is to pick up the picture, but if I do, I know Keith will suck me into this conversation he's having with Coach Sullivan. Instead, I stare at it lying face down in the dirt, knowing it's so close but seems far away . . . kind of like my ball career.

Keith walks over and scoops the photo up. He turns it over in his hands and uses the bottom of his UC San Diego T-shirt to clean it off. It's the second time today someone has kept me from permanently dumping moments from the past. He stares at the kid in the photo like he doesn't even know him. Maybe that's true. The only times we speak to each other is when we're arguing or calling each other asshole. Keith used to be the guy I went to when I needed advice about girls or a good cover to get out of the house for a party. He even took me to my first kegger. These days all he does is play bad cop and yell at me when I haven't finished a paper.

"Sorry about that." I hear him say to Coach Sullivan.

The old guy shrugs. "I'm a coach; I see family meltdowns on and off the field every day."

Keith attempts to laugh but it comes out hollow. He taps the photo on his palm. "We actually came out here looking for our dad." Coach Sullivan looks puzzled. "I don't mean today, literally, but maybe you saw him pass through at some point recently?" Keith pulls a second photo out of his pocket. It's the one of my parents at their anniversary dinner in Napa Valley.

The coach takes it and studies it carefully. I pull my earphones out of my ears to listen. I've almost forgotten why we're here. Not to make me feel shitty about the ball career I screwed up, but to find the man who once convinced me to play the game.

"I can't say that I have; I'm sorry," the coach says. "And I'm here most days with my team, so I would be the one to see him." He hands the picture back to Keith.

Keith doesn't put the photo away. "Are you sure? We think he headed this way. Might have even been a few months ago. He drives a dark blue Camaro."

Keith may have stopped playing ball by the sixth grade, but the one thing he did like to do with my dad was fiddle around with engines. They fixed up that Camaro together. Keith used to joke that working on a carburetor was good practice for fixing up somebody's heart. I'd sit in the garage and watch the two of them study how-to books and watch videos like grease monkeys trying to figure out how to get parts to work.

"You know what?" the coach says suddenly. "Come to think of it, I do remember something strange several months back."

I can't stop myself. I stuff my earphones in my pocket and walk over to them. They both notice me coming because I almost get creamed by a few bike riders zooming by. Keith doesn't say anything, though, when I safely make my way to where they're standing. I cross my arms across my chest and listen in.

"I had to cancel practice due to a rainstorm and remember there was a man sitting in the bleachers, just looking out, paying no attention to the downpour."

"You think it was him?" I blurt out.

Coach Sullivan scratches his head. "Can't say. Didn't get a good look. But if it was, he probably would've headed up Route Ten. Thirty-three was closed because of a mudslide."

Keith grabs the guy's hand and shakes it vigorously. "Thanks. Thanks a lot."

"Good luck, I hope you find him," the coach says before turning to point a finger at me. "And you—if God gave you that gift of an arm, you'd be a fool to waste it."

"Yes, sir," I say and nod.

I hear another *clink* and watch the kid hit a foul as the coach walks away. The ball rolls in our direction and stops at Keith's feet. He picks it up and starts to walk away to give the ball back to them. God forbid he actually throw the thing, might hurt his precious lifesaving hands. I stand and watch the kid get ready to hit another ball.

"Hey, Jay, let's go someplace that has nothing to do with baseball," Keith says.

I'm about to say I couldn't agree more when Keith hurls the ball at my head at top speed. Instinctively, I reach up and catch it. "Hey, watch it!" Then I send the ball right back to him, curling up and throwing a fastball before he can even react. He reaches out to grab the ball, but it bounces off his hand.

"Ouch!" Keith shakes it out.

I can't help but smirk. "That's what you get," I say and walk past him.

Keith's reply is so soft I'm sure he doesn't think I hear him. "That's what I wanted."

11// WHITNEY

I feel like such an idiot. All this time I've been worrying about my own problems with the She-Bitches and the lie heard 'round the world that I forgot I'm not the only Connolly in pain here. Yes, Keith, Lexi, Jason, and I have our issues, but somehow we've all dropped the ball when it comes to looking after Sam. We're all he has in this world till we figure out where Dad disappeared to. And how do we help him handle it all?

By pretty much ignoring him completely.

Yep, it's official: we suck as a family unit.

I run down the narrow path and almost get barreled over by a guy on a bike towing a blue carriage behind it. I hear two girls squealing giddily inside as they pass. This is probably not the safest place for me to walk. I veer off the path and try to put myself in Sam's shoes. Where would I go if I were him? He'd prefer to sit by a fountain or a park sculpture, that's for sure, but since this place is nowhere near as nice as Griffith Park, I'm thinking the likelihood of a sculpture like the Astronomers Monument being around are slim to none. He doesn't have his bike with him. Hmm . . . a bunch of boys in soccer uniforms kick a ball past my head and I duck to keep from getting hit.

"We just played for at least an hour," a sweaty little boy whines. "Let's go to the park!"

Park! I notice a swing set in the distance. Sam once fell off the monkey bars and broke his right arm, so I'm not sure the park is his favorite in the world, but when his options are a bench covered in bird poop or a swing set, I'm thinking I'll find him on the swing set. I walk across the muddy field from last night's rain and to the entrance of the park covered in Astro turf. The place is pretty much deserted except for the swings and the large sandbox that has ride-on diggers in it. A few mothers are pushing toddlers on baby swings, but the regular swings are empty. Except for one. I'm relieved to see Sam going back and forth slowly, the photo box and his sketchpad balanced precariously on his lap. He's completely in a trance, staring down at his feet, which he's dragging through the sand. I'm so happy to see him. I want to sprint to his side, but I don't want to spook him.

I move slowly, and out of the corner of my eye, I notice the seesaws on the other end of the park. Lexi is sitting hunched over on one end of a seesaw. Behind her, I notice Zak approaching. Lexi has someone who has her back. I focus on my little brother, so I can have his back too. Almost as if sensing I'm there, Sam looks up. I expect him to be angry to see me. Instead, his oval-shaped eyes, so similar to my own, remind me of a puppy in a store window. I just want to squeeze the kid.

I sit down on the swing next to him and push off. "Want to talk about it?"

Sam shrugs. He opens the photo box and stares at the stack of pictures inside. "I don't remember half these things we did." He picks up one of us at Disneyland. "I was too young I guess." He looks at me and his brow creases with concern. "All I remember is Mom and Dad fighting a lot."

"Mom and Dad didn't fight a lot," I say almost accusingly and then stop myself. These are Sam's memories, not mine. "I mean, I can't believe that's what you remember."

He laughs to himself. "Great memories, huh?"

Gently, I take the box from his hands and place it on my own lap. I slow my swing to a stop and look through for something that will spark his memory in a good way. "We can do better than fights. Let's see . . ." I pull out a picture of Mom climbing a wooden barricade. She's wearing war paint on her cheeks and a bandana with her company name on it. *Think Whitney*, I tell myself. *Where is this from? Oh, I know!*

"Remember this?" I ask, showing Sam. "This is from that time Mom signed us all up for some family challenge on her company's retreat. We spent the entire weekend smelly and disgusting on obstacle courses. We were terrible! Keith face-planted when he fell trying to climb up one of those rope ladders. Lexi kept tripping every time she had to run, and then Jason would swoop in and try to save her like he was her power twin or something. Dad had to carry you and me because we were the youngest. You and I loved it," I tell him.

"We did?" Sam asks, biting his lip. I can almost see the wheels turning as he tries to unlock the door to this memory.

"Yep, and Mom was the worst of all. She just laughed herself silly every time one of us screwed up. When we finally got to the obstacle course wall, which is this picture here, suddenly you got this look in your eye. You were determined for us to finish the course, even though there was no way we could win at that point. You told us to imagine we were all Spider-Man. You were obsessed with him. You even went first over the wall." I grab Sam's leg as I remember the feeling of watching him scale that high platform. "You got to the top in no time and captured the flag that was up there. We were all cheering." I pull my swing over to his and lock my left leg around his right one so we're attached. "You were the big hero of the day. You even got a reward—"

Sam interrupts me. "A twelve-scoop banana split."

"That's right!" I'm excited he actually remembers. His face

breaks into a huge smile. "Remember Mom had one too? Extra chocolate, marshmallows and—"

"Pineapple!" Sam finishes. I don't remember the last time I saw him this excited. The breeze blows that mop of brown hair out of his eyes, and the two of us just stare at each other for a moment, remembering the sights and sounds of that day. "Thanks," he says shyly. "I remember that now."

"Good." I look down at the sketchbook in his hands. I wonder if I should keep going with this bonding thing since it seems to be working. "So I hear your teacher selected you for the county art show next week."

"How did you hear that?" Sam's eyebrows go up.

I don't tell him the truth. His art teacher, Mr. Colligan, who's also my art teacher, stopped me the other day and asked if any of us were going to come see his show. I didn't even know Sam was in it. "Your teacher says you're some sort of art genius, which I find hard to believe." He knocks his swing into mine. "But I'm willing to give you the benefit of the doubt till the show, at least." I nod to his sketchpad. "Want to show me something award-worthy?"

Sam pulls his pad off his lap and hides it behind his back. "No way."

"Come on," I beg. I put the photo box down and start to swing again. As great as that memory of our family trip was, it also makes me depressed. There will never be a family trip like that again. I try not to dwell on it, but it's hard not to blink back tears. I don't want my brother to see me cry. Not when I'm here trying to cheer *him* up. I have to focus on my breathing, like my psychiatrist says I should in situations like this. "*Breathe in and out. In and out. Concentrate on something else,*" I can hear him say.

"Show me where you get your inspiration from," I suggest to Sam.

But it's already too late. I can feel my medication kick in and the swing set does a complete 360 before righting itself and bursting into a rainbow of colors that are as comforting to me as a hot cocoa with extra marshmallows.

"I just draw things," Sam says, starting to swing again a little. "Stuff that will take me away from this reality, you know?"

Maybe Sam and I have more in common than I realized. "Trust me, I know." I nod to the book he has tucked under his arm as he swings. "So why don't you show me some of your work."

Sam stops swinging again and passes me his sketchbook. I open it slowly, afraid of what I'm going to see. What if he sucks and I have to lie to him about it?

Thankfully when I turn to the first page, I know I'm so wrong to even think that. This is no kiddie drawing. Sam's used soft charcoal pencils to draw a meadow beneath a starry night sky and every star, every flower, every blade of grass is so vivid it nearly jumps off the page. I do a double take when I look at my brother again. How did I not notice my brother was an artist? How many times have I passed an art project in a hallway at school and never realized Sam's signature was along the bottom?

I look down at a painting of a tiger and the song Jason was blasting in his earphones sneaks into my thoughts. Capital Cities' "Safe and Sound" sums up exactly what Sam is trying to do when he escapes into his artwork. I know because it's the same thing that happens when I let the hallucinations take over, like they are right now.

The tiger sprouts vines from his head in a multitude of colors. Pink palm tress and lilac mountains appear behind the swing set. Then Sam takes my hand and we jump *Mary Poppins*–style into his sketchbook. He uses an oversize crayon to draw a scene in the scene in a jungle for us to walk through. Bumblebees and insects fly by as I use binoculars to view the world he created up close. Green pops on the tree vines and flowers seemingly open as we pass them, bathing the jungle in reds, pinks, and whites.

Sam points to a house atop a pyramid that he's just drawn and the two of us begin to climb it. Atop the mountain is a city that Sam draws for us to ride through on a motorcycle. I feel my hair fly behind me as we tear through the city on the bike. Sam keeps singing about how he could keep us safe and sound as he paints object after object. The two of us are laughing and all I can think about is how this feels like we're on a tropical island somewhere in the Caribbean. I never want to go home again if this is what life is like on an island.

I grab Sam's hand again and give it a tight squeeze. As I do, I feel myself get sucked out of his painting and back onto the swings. I want to cry out for a moment to stop reality from taking over again. That world my brother created—that I created through my hallucination—was a beautiful, happy one. But the boy behind those paintings is right here on the swing next to me and I know now I should never let him go. It's my job to make *him* feel safe and sound. Not his to make me feel that way. Maybe it's our job to help each other; we're brother and sister after all.

I hand Sam back his sketchbook, pausing to look at a multi-colored dragon he's drawn. He places the book on top of the photo box on the ground. The two of us pump our legs at the same time and begin to soar into the cool air. Our hair lifts up and starts to fly around us. I can barely see Sam's eyes anymore, but I know he's looking at me and wondering what I'm thinking.

"Sam, you're incredible! Why didn't you ever tell us how good you were?"

Sam's cheeks color as he climbs higher. "I knew you'd all figure it out on your own. Eventually."

I start to laugh and he joins in. We keep pumping our legs till our swings go so high it feels like we could touch the sky.

12 //
LEXI

Sam may have been the first one off the field, but I struck out seconds later.

I was halfway down the bike path before I realized I had no clue where I was going.

What else was new?

It's one thing for your twin to call you trashy. We shared a womb, so Jason can get away with trading barbs with me that other people can't. Besides, I dish it out pretty good myself.

But when your baby brother basically calls you a clown and doesn't realize he actually means something much worse, it gets to you.

"On your left!" I hear a bicyclist bark seconds before barreling me down. I jump backward and almost wind up in the bushes. Two more bikes zoom by right behind the first followed by a pack of rollerblading girls before I realize I need a new, safer place to sulk.

I cut through the bushes—seems smarter than staying on the maniac cyclist path—and spot a playground a few yards off. I can hear the sounds of laughter and squealing all the way from here. There's a bunch of moms and toddlers overrunning the sandbox and the swings area, but the see-saws are pretty much deserted. I guess they're all washed up. Just like me.

I sit down at one end and pull my compact out of my bag. The sun bounces off the mirror and makes me squint for a second before my face comes into view. My brown eyes are heavily made up in smoky shades of gray and black, both above and below my eye, which is also outlined in a thick black liner and three coats of black mascara. I barely recognize the girl I'm looking at. Maybe that was the point after Mom died. I wanted to be in anyone's skin but my own. Sam didn't have that luxury. It turns out he didn't have anybody. Jason stopped playing ball. Whit's shoulder to lean on became her therapist. God, I've been a crappy sister.

I rummage around my bag till I find the eye makeup remover wipes that I go through like breath mints. The sounds of the swings squeaking back and forth nearby almost lull me to sleep; I'm so exhausted. But then I hear a kid screech when his mom pushes him too high, and I jolt back awake and remember what I'm doing. Using the compact as a guide, I slowly wipe away my upper lid shadow, being careful not to smudge the liner at the same time (a girl can't survive without at least eyeliner). Then I do the other eye. I stare into the mirror and blink a few times to make sure the face I'm looking at is really my own. I never look into the mirror at night after I wash it. Here, in the bright light of morning, on a playground seesaw, there is no escaping me.

Hi ya, old Lexi. It's been a while.

Thump! The seesaw goes flying upward and I grab the sides to hang on, dropping my compact in the dirt in the process. I look over and see Zak sitting down on the other end. He gives me a shit-eating grin, and I consider picking my compact up and bouncing light off the mirror to blind him. Instead, I shoot him death rays.

He isn't bothered by my glare a bit. "The little dude got to you, huh?"

I lean back and almost upend myself. "No." I reach down and grab the compact, dusting it off instead of looking at Zak. I freaking hate how the guy can read me like a book. "The wind blew dirt in my eye. I walked off to find a bathroom so I could flush it out." I push off with my feet and Zak allows the seesaw to glide into the air. For a few minutes, we just enjoy the ride. Up, down. Up, down. But I can't shake the look he's giving me. His eyes never leave my face, and I feel the heat rush into my cheeks. I wish I could make the color stop, just like I wish I could stop sneaking glances at the boy across from me. He's looking at me like I'm a cross between someone he needs to save and someone he wants to elope with in Vegas. I'm not sure which is worse.

When Zak's feet hit the ground again, he holds the seesaw there and I'm held prisoner in the air. My body is pulled forward and my legs dangle helplessly. There's nothing I can do, but focus on him as he hoarsely blurts out, "Lexi, it's just me here, okay? You can tell me anything." I glance down at the washed-out red wood on the seesaw and think about how easy it would be to get a splinter if I ran my finger along the grain. It's impossible not to hear him when he adds, "I'm here for you. You know that, right? So tell me what you're thinking."

There's a part of me that wants to spill my guts to him. Lay it all out in big, bold letters and skywriting and all that other shit. But when I look back and see Zak's face, all I see is pity. The same pity my mom's friends give me when they pass me in the supermarket. The same look the guidance counselor shoots me when I say college isn't even on my radar. The exact expression Whitney's psychiatrist flashes me when I pick up my sister from an appointment. They think I'm a total screwup just like Sam does. And they're right.

"I thought I said to leave me alone." My voice sounds like sandpaper. I wait for Zak to argue. Instead I feel the seesaw drop and I hold on to the bar for dear life as the seat hits the dirt and I almost bounce off it. When I look up, he's already walking away. "Wait, *what the*?"

Zak turns around. The look he gives me this time is anything but pitiful. It's angry. "You're acting like a total bitch, Lexi, and you know what? I'm finally over it." He disappears down the path, sidestepping two kids racing by on scooters.

I stare at his retreating frame. I should scream. Shout. Run in front of Zak and stop him with my own hands. But I don't. This time, I've gone too far and I'm too ashamed to do anything about it. "God, I am a bitch," I mumble.

I don't know how long I sit there hating myself before I get off the seesaw, grab the compact that dropped again, and head back to the car. Keith, Whitney, and Sam are already there. I glance quickly in the car and see Jason talking quietly with Zak in the backseat. He doesn't look up.

"So what did you find out?" Whitney asks Keith.

"The coach says there was a man fitting Dad's description here a few months back." Keith stares at the photo of Mom and Dad's anniversary. "He was just sitting in the bleachers during a downpour." Keith shakes his head. "The coach says it might have been Dad."

"Really?" Sam sounds so excited, my heart might split into two.

Bitchy Lexi would take this moment to shoot Sam down so that's exactly what I don't do. "Did he see which way this guy went?"

Keith looks hopefully at me. "His best guess was down

Route Ten. Thirty-three was closed because of a mudslide."

"Excellent!" Sam jumps up and down. "You said Route Ten was where we used to camp, right?" Whitney nods. "Then let's go!"

"All right then. You heard, Sam. Let's load up the car and go!" Keith puts his hands on Sam's shoulders and steers him back toward the car.

Whitney and I just stand there and watch until Sam is tucked inside.

"Do you really think it was Dad?" she asks me, her brown eyes big and wide and way too innocent for this conversation.

I glance at Zak again, wishing he would look up so I could smile at him. Then maybe he'd smile back and things would be right again. As right as they ever could be when all we do is bicker.

I choose my words carefully. "Statistically, it's probably not Dad." Whitney's face falls. "But . . . I'm going to be more optimistic from here on out, so yes. It was definitely Dad."

Her face breaks into a wide grin. The grin I'm still hoping Zak will flash me when we get into the car. The one I hope Sam will give me again when I prove to him that I'm a sister worth having. When I show Keith I'm not a total screwup. When I prove to Jason I'm a twin he can be happy to have. A smile from Whitney is a good start.

I slide into the empty passenger seat next to Keith and listen to the engine rev to life again. "Let's go," I say and we're off.

13 //
KEITH

When we pull up to Emmet State Park, I breathe a huge sigh of relief.

At least something in our lives hasn't changed.

The rustic campground looks exactly like we left it. Towering coastal redwood trees (that as a kid reminded me of *Star Wars's* moon of Endor) still dot the landscape as far as the eye can see. Wood cabins and yurts are lined up along the river next to fire pits. In the distance, I see the familiar RV site area, the playground, and the camp store and laundry facilities. But it's the large wood cabin home on the hill that I'm most curious about. Last time we were here a few years back, it belonged to the camp's longtime owners, the Carraghers.

I hear the leather seats crinkle and turn around. Whitney is leaning over the third row, watching Jason. He's staring at a photograph and I don't have to see it to know which one it is. There was a batch of photos of us camping here, but one sticks out in my mind as much as it does his—us with the Carragher sisters.

"She'll probably be here," Whitney sings, her voice lighter

than I've heard it in a while. "But I bet her dad won't be too happy to see you."

Jason grimaces, but doesn't say anything. He's been quiet for the last forty-five minutes it took to get up here. Zak leans over, looks at the photograph, and whistles. "They're hot," he says and Lexi's head almost spins off its axis. "Who are they?"

"Rachel and Anna Carragher," Whitney explains, her voice giddy. "Jason dated Rachel every summer. Her dad caught them skinny dipping two summers ago."

"Eww, skinny dipping?" Sam asks. "Why would anyone want to do that?"

I stroke the scruff growing in on my chin. Skinny dipping is nothing compared to what I was doing with Anna.

"It was Keith's idea," Jason says, sounding defensive. "He said he'd warn me if anyone was coming."

Lexi and Whitney both smack me in the head. "Hey!" I duck to get out of their line of fire. "In my defense, I was much younger and not a responsible caretaker like I am now." Whitney gives me a look. "I was distracted back then."

"Is that the trip you lost your virginity?" Jason pipes up.

"What? No!" I stammer while they all continue to stare at me. Zak gives me a thumbs-up and sly smile. "I . . . this is not a topic of discussion!" They all burst out laughing, even Sam. "I hate you all." I think this is one of those moments when I'm supposed to be parental. "Everyone out of the car!" I bark, sounding more like Dad.

I'm out first, mostly so I can avoid them seeing how flush my face is. I hope the cool mountain air brings my cheeks back to a normal temperature. I put my hands on my hips and look around at the familiar patch of dirt, fire pit, rickety grill, and utility hookups. "Here we are. Site forty-four. Our usual."

Whitney walks around for a moment before grabbing a long twig and poking it in the darkened fire pit. "Doesn't look like anyone's been here in a while."

"Did you think Dad would just magically be here when we showed up?" Jason huffs.

"No." Whitney pushes her hair out of her face and kicks some dirt around, looking like a bull about to charge. "I just meant it isn't really camping season right now."

"All right, all right." I put my hands up in a sign of peace before another Connolly civil war breaks out. "Let's set up camp and then we can spread out and ask if anyone's seen him. Sound good?"

Everyone nods and we head to the car to unload our camping equipment. Sam grabs the sleeping bags, Lexi takes the pillows, Whitney hauls out the cooler, and I feel a pit of dread in my stomach when I see Jason and Zak lift out the tent. I don't remember ever putting this thing together without Dad's help. The guys drop it on the ground with a *thud* and I roll the tent around.

"I don't think there are any directions on this thing, are there?" I ask sheepishly.

Zak scratches his head. "You mean you guys don't know how to put up a tent? I thought you went camping every summer?"

"It's been a while." I pull several different sized poles out of their compartment and look at them like they're from a foreign planet. "We'll figure it out, I'm sure."

Jason doesn't look convinced and with good reason. We have no clue what we're doing. We get the yellow old-school tent up in minutes. Lexi declares the boys can sleep in that one. But a half hour later, we look like we're playing a game of Twister with the other tent. Lexi's inside the friggin' thing, on her hands and knees, trying to hold down the corners. Sam is doing the same from the outside. The poles are in, but every time Whitney and Jason try to bend them in place, they pop back. I'm messing with a jammed zipper on the mesh door and getting nowhere.

"Here, maybe I can hold it with my foot," Lexi says and spreads her legs out wide to stand on two corners. Zak does the same in the opposite corners.

"And I'll anchor it with my arm," Sam suggests. He lies down and looks like he's posing with his elbow, propping up his head and the tent.

This does nothing because as soon as I push the tent poles back in on one side and Whitney does the same on the other, the whole thing starts to lean like the Tower of Pisa.

"Whoa! It's falling!" Zak yells. "It's coming down."

"I got it! I got it!" Whitney says trying to hold up two poles while the tent crumbles around her. She can't stop giggling.

"No, you don't!" Jason is the only one being serious. "You have to put the poles into the holes and then clip the—"

"Clip the what?" I ask. "Do you mean the zipper?" I pull at the zipper again and realize I'm tearing the mesh. "Ah! Zipper stuck! Zipper stuck!" I yank harder and the tent falls farther. "Abandon ship!"

From somewhere inside the tent, I hear Sam yell, "Save yourself!"

"I'm not leaving you behind," Lexi says with a laugh and pulls Sam out before the tent collapses on them both.

The two of them are in hysterics and I start in as well. Whitney leans on me, she's laughing so hard, and I put my arm around her. Zak has his head in his hands and he groans miserably, but I can tell he's cracking up too. It feels good to not be screaming at each other for a change. Not to see everyone walking around like we're at a daily funeral. For the moment, we're happy to be around each other. Then I look at Jason. His face is made of stone. "Relax," I say and put a hand on his shoulder. "We'll try again."

Jason shrugs me off. "I don't do tents. I was on campfire duty with Mom."

I run my hand through my hair. You can't please everyone. "Okay then," I say and can't help but sigh. "Go set up the campfire."

"I will," Jason huffs. "Anything to get away from you guys," he says under his breath.

Thankfully, the others don't hear him. Sam is reenacting the tent falling by sticking his head inside and then collapsing to the floor.

"Excuse me? Do you have a permit for the night?"

When I turn around a girl in a park ranger jacket and hat is staring at me. The outfit may scare people off, but I know the girl underneath it. The brown eyes, long, straight blonde hair, the button nose. I couldn't forget her face even if I tried. "Anna?"

Her stern expression softens. I see her pink lips spread into a slow grin. "Keith? Oh my God! What are you doing here?" She jogs over and pulls me into a hug and I smell the welcome, familiar scent of lavender soap. She must still use the stuff. I once mailed her a case of Yardley lavender soap after the summer. For some reason, the fact that she still uses it makes me happy.

"It's so good to see you," I say, my arms still wrapped around her small waist. My hand has somehow made its way under her shirt slightly and I can feel her skin. My own skin warms slightly. I pull my hand away, aware the others are watching. I clear my throat. "I was just going to find your dad. I know we should have gotten a permit weeks ago. I'm sorry."

Seeing Lexi, Whitney, and Sam, Anna gives a little wave. She pulls out a clipboard, suddenly all business again. "I'm afraid you'll have to make do with me. Dad retired last year."

"What?" I say in surprise. "Your dad is a workaholic."

Anna's smile fades and she looks down at her work boots, which have mud splattered on them. "Yeah, well, the stroke slowed him down."

I instantly feel like an ass. "Geez, I'm sorry. I didn't know."

She shrugs. "It is what it is."

It is what it is. Anna sounds a lot like me.

"Luckily, this site is free so I can give you a permit right now." Suddenly the radio hanging off her belt buckle crackles to life.

"Anna?" The voice on the line has static. "We need you up on the west ridge."

Anna pulls the radio off her waist and presses a button. The static goes silent. "Be there in ten." She looks at me sadly. "I've got to run."

"You should go with her," Lexi blurts out.

The two of us look at each other. Anna's cheeks are as red as her T-shirt. My sister is trying to set me up. I give her a look.

"I just mean, you haven't seen each other in a while," Lexi says while Zak watches her curiously. "You two should catch up."

"You can come along if you want," Anna says. "I could use the company."

"We'll be fine here," Whitney adds.

Anna looks at me hopefully and I crack. I could never resist her full lips and that smell. . . . I'm going to smell lavender in my sleep. "All right, I'll walk with you for a bit."

Anna smiles. "Great." She looks at Lexi. "You guys keep a lookout for bears."

I stop short. "You know I hate bears."

She laughs. "As I recall, they're not too fond of you either."

Anna leads the way along a trail that runs along the water. If I'm right, up ahead should be a bunch of boulders and a waterfall that feeds into a larger pool. That's the site of Jason's infamous skinny-dipping session that was interrupted by Mr. Carragher. I was supposed to be on watch, but I was too busy getting to second base with Anna underneath some brush near a big redwood tree. I was just glad he didn't find us too. My hand on his daughter's boob wouldn't have gone over well.

When we reach the waterfall, I can't help but stop and listen to the sound of rushing water. This was always my favorite spot at the campgrounds. Even before I learned I could make out at Emmet State Park, I'd come here to listen to music on my iPod, or write whatever short-lived girlfriend I had some pathetic love-note postcard. I'd disappear for hours to get away from my family who felt way too suffocating in one pop-up tent. Funny how now I'd give anything to go back to that time and place.

"Penny for your thoughts," Anna says and I can't help but smile. She's been saying that dorky expression since we were ten.

"I'm just thinking about how cool it would be to be fifteen again," I reply. "No one in my family was pissed at me back then."

"Interesting." Anna's watching me closely as I climb onto another boulder a little higher up than the firs. I hold out my hand to help her up. "That bad, huh? I'll show you my scars if you show me yours." She takes a seat on the rock and I sit down next to her.

"Deal." I can't take my eyes off her even in that crappy park ranger getup. At least I know what she looks like with it off. Man, was she always this hot? Her boobs have definitely grown in. I wish I could get beyond second base with her now.

"You go first," she says and nudges me with her elbow.

Back to reality. I fill Anna in on the last year. Watching her face rise and fall makes me feel like I'm reliving the grief and drama all over again. Thankfully, we can commiserate. Like me, she had to leave behind a career she loved to help the family (in this case, with the business). When Anna gets to the part about her dad's stroke and how it happened, I can hardly believe it. Her dad did triathlons. He was more fit than anyone I knew. By the time I'm telling her about the cops looking for a guy that fits my dad's description, the two of us are practically sitting on top of each other, we're so close. Her hands are woven with mine.

"I'm sorry, I wish I could say I've seen your dad, but I haven't," she says softly.

Her lips are so close to mine right now, I can hardly think of anything else. Must concentrate. "It was a long shot."

"If he was the man in the bleachers at the ball park, by the time he got up here, the campgrounds would've been closed and all the roads leading here washed out."

I feel her fingers stroke mine. Breathe. I look at the waterfall again. "So maybe he just kept heading north on the main road and skipped the campgrounds."

When I look at Anna again, she's nodding pensively. "Yeah, that seems most likely." She tightens her grip on my hands and her brown eyes pop dramatically. "You know, when my dad's feeling run-down, he always wants to go someplace where he feels like a kid. A place that helps him recharge. Maybe that's what your dad's looking for."

The thought of him relieving his youth when it should be me enjoying mine bothers me. Without thinking, I pull away and lean back on the boulder with my elbows. "Could be."

Anna doesn't let me get away. She lies down next to me so that we're side by side. She looks at me. Why does she have to smell so good? "God, life did not turn out the way we planned, did it?"

I laugh bitterly. "You're supposed to be living in Manhattan by now," I remind her.

She looks away, focusing on the swirling, bubbling water beneath the waterfall. "Trust me, I know. I actually made it to Manhattan for a while. Did you know that?" I shake my head. Anna's whole face lights up. "I lived in a loft in SoHo with five roommates. It was so crowded and we had zero privacy, but I loved it." Her smile fades. "But when Dad needed me back here . . ." Her voice trails off and I sigh.

I know the story too well. As much as it sucks to have Anna's life turn out to be as disastrous as my own, it feels good to finally have someone who gets what I'm going through. It makes me wish we had more than just one night together. "I wish I could have warned the younger me."

"What would you have told him? That we were naively stupid to want our own lives?" She picks at a small dandelion somehow growing between a crack in the rock we're sitting on. "Now we've got the wisdom of our midtwenties and are so much smarter," she adds sarcastically.

The wind blows in my direction and the smell of lavender is overwhelming. So is the feeling running through my body. God, I want her. Right here in the open on a rock, no less. I lean over so that I'm practically on top of her. "I'm pretty sure we're still supposed to be making stupid decisions," I whisper as her nose brushes mine.

"You're right." She doesn't pull away. "We should be partying all night."

My nose brushes hers again. Just a little closer . . . "Wasted out of our minds."

Anna's eyes lock on my own. "One-night stands."

I don't flinch. My lips brush hers lightly. "Awkward morning-after breakfasts."

She closes her eyes. "I miss being young."

Her voice is so sad, I hesitate kissing her, but I can't stop myself. I press my lips against hers, feeling the warmth return to my body as she kisses me back. I'm not sure how long we lie there kissing, like two crazy teens, before I do something radical. I pull her hand and begin sliding her off the rock into the water. Our feet hit the water and she screeches, but I can tell she likes where I'm going with this. She pulls off her park ranger jacket and I pull off my T-shirt. For a moment, I feel like we're being watched, but when I quickly scan the tree line and the boulders, I don't see anything. For a moment, I'm off duty. I can relax. Have fun with a beautiful girl who seems to want to do the same thing I do. I motion to the waterfall. Unlike Jason, I never got to skinny dip here.

"So let's be young again!" I begin removing my shoes and socks excitedly. I throw them on the shoreline. "Just for a little while at least."

Anna's already untying her heavy boots, but her eyes remain on mine. "I thought you'd never ask."

14 //
JASON

What are we doing here? Did anyone really think we'd pull up to one of these places on the Connolly memory train and Dad would just be waiting? "Hey, kids! I was hoping you'd come find me! Let's go home!"

God, I sound bitter. I *am* bitter. I can't help it. While the others have their little ABC Family sitcom moment back there putting up the tent, I'm keeping it real. We came, he's not here, let's move on. But no, they want to stay and do what? Roast marshmallows? Give me a break. We're not a TV movie. This is real life and ours right now sucks. Why are Keith and the others trying to pretend otherwise?

I reach a clearing between the redwood trees and scream as loud as I can. My voice bounces off imaginary caverns and hits me in the face. There. That felt better. I don't even care if the others heard me. Let them think I've been attacked by a bear. Okay, maybe that's harsh. I imagine Sam running down the path screaming my name and now I feel crappy. I'll head back and let them know I'm okay after I gather firewood for our camp-fire. But if they think I'm going to sit around and sing "Kumbaya" and all that shit, they're mistaken. I push through the brush and start gathering whatever twigs and small logs I can find. I hear footsteps behind me. Yep, it's got to be Sam. Or maybe it's our family spy. I roll my eyes when I think of Whitney harping on me.

"Go away." I gather as much wood as I can carry in my arms. "I've got this."

"Well, that's not a very nice hello."

I turn around so fast some of the twigs fly out of my arms. I'd recognize that flirty voice anywhere. "Rachel?"

My skinny-dipping partner is standing on the path in front of me and she looks every bit as hot as she did when we were caught two years ago. I take that back. She looks hotter. Her waist is so small I could cup it with my two hands and my fingers would touch, and she's still got that gloriously long blonde hair that I adore. Her shorts are shorter than ever, and she's wearing a hot pink velour hoodie that has me wondering what's underneath it. She bats her hazel eyes at me.

"How are you, Jay?" She walks toward me and I feel like a deer caught in headlights. I can't move. All I can do is watch her hips. "My sister texted me the Connollys were at their old campsite."

"Yep. We are." Ugh. Is that all I could come up with? Lame, lame, lame.

"Your parents finally dragged you guys back out here." Rachel looks amazed. Were her eyes always that light? They look almost yellow in the afternoon sun. "How is everyone?"

My back stiffens. For a moment, I just want to forget. "They're good," I lie. "Same old, same old. Nothing's really changed."

"Same here." Rachel's fingers tighten around a clunky two-way radio near her belt buckle. If I'm not mistaken, she switches the power to off. Rachel points to the twigs in my arms. "That's a pathetic pile of wood you have there. Come on," she motions for me to follow her. "I'll help you gather some real firewood, city boy."

Oh man, look at that ass. It's even more perky and round than I remembered. Who could say no to following her? I walk along behind her like a lost puppy.

"So," Rachel begins as she veers off the path and into the woods. She squats a bug that lands on her forearm with a loud *THWACK!* "Where'd you decide to go?"

She's staring at me and I'm thinking of how she looked in that waterfall, her hair all wet, her skin glistening . . . man, I miss that waterfall. Wait. She just asked me something, didn't she? What was it? Oh yeah. I didn't understand the question. "Go?"

"Yeah, to college," she says as if it should be obvious, but I'm too busy looking at the sprinkle of freckles on her cheeks. "Junior year! Time to think about these things, although last time we saw each other you were bragging about how you'd get offers from no less than ten colleges to play baseball." My heart sinks at the words "college" and "baseball." "Have you been recruited yet? Did you pick Ivy League or a state school?"

I stare at an inchworm dangling from a string near her head. "I haven't decided yet."

"Did your team ever make it to the high school world series or whatever they call it?" she asks.

Rachel looks so happy for me, I can't burst her bubble. Besides, I like her version of me better right now. "Of course! We won too. It was a hell of a night."

She shakes her head and I watch her hair move like it's in slow motion. "You lead a charmed life, Jason Connolly." Her eyes narrow and her smile turns playful. "The question is: Do you still know how to have fun?" She moves deeper into the trees where I can only see the top of her head and calls me with her finger.

I freeze. "Your dad will kill me."

Her smile wavers for a moment, but I'm not sure why. "Trust me, you're fine." She pulls off her velour jacket and leaves it hanging on a branch. Underneath, she's wearing a tight, pale pink tank top that leaves nothing to the imagination.

I smile to myself. *You know what, Keith? Maybe camping wasn't such a bad idea after all.*

"Come on, city boy, let's go get wet," Rachel says coyly. She stops walking when she sees what I assume is a goofy look on my face. God, I hope I'm not drooling. "Unless you forgot how to play the game."

Skinny dipping? She doesn't have to ask me twice. I begin unbuttoning my shirt immediately. "I've still got plenty of game off the field as well."

Cheesy line, yes, but it's obviously effective. Rachel pulls me into the foliage where the two of us begin to run toward that waterfall I remember and don't look back.

15 // WHITNEY

Eww! Gross!

I will never, ever, EVER spy on my brothers again. EVER!

It was getting dark so I left the campsite to go and tell them we were ready to eat and I found them . . . I found them . . . EWW! Oh God, I saw Keith's tongue down Anna's throat! And Jason . . . his shirt was open and he was hooking up with Rachel. Watching your brothers get busy is worse than seeing your parents kiss. Maybe that's because young people are better at the makeout thing, so it feels like you're watching a porno or something.

All I know is that I was so freaked out that my hallucinations kicked into high gear and suddenly Keith and Jason were singing One Direction's "Kiss You." Jason would rather die than be seen singing One Direction, so if that wasn't weird enough, then I saw pixie dust flying around the darkened night sky and all these foxes and bears came out to sing along with them. They were oversize animals with giant papier-mâché heads like I was in some sort of carnival. It was so bizarre; I'm sure I'm going to have nightmares tonight.

Jason's hand was on Rachel's boob! Gross!

I'm still shuddering and mumbling to myself when I stumble back on our campsite. I appear from behind so the group doesn't even realize I'm back. Sam is lying on the picnic table eating gooey s'mores while Lexi and Zak are roasting marshmallows, their heads so close they're practically attached.

Oh no. Are these two going to make out too?

I stop short, afraid I'm about to witness another sibling moment I'd rather forget. Sam, cover your eyes!

Lexi and Zak stick their marshmallows in the fire at the same time.

"Sorry." Lexi is sort of quiet. "You go first."

"No, you go," Zak insists.

They both find a way to roast their marshmallows at the same time and all I can hear is the crackling and popping of the fire, which illuminates their bodies with an eerie red glow.

"So . . . do you like camping?" Lexi asks, sounding as awkward and tense as I usually do.

Zak looks at her. "Do I like camping?" he repeats. Lexi shrugs. "So we're doing small talk now?"

"I'm trying," Lexi says softly, and Zak sighs.

"Okay, I hate camping." He emphasizes the word *hate*. Lexi starts to laugh. "I'm serious! I'm not a fan of bugs or snakes and I've read people eat like four bugs a year in your sleep. Why add to that number?"

Lexi laughs harder. "That's not true, is it?"

"Would I ever lie to you?" Zak is dead serious.

The fire pops and hisses as their heads move closer. I feel like I'm watching a movie.

Time to press the Pause button.

"Hi!" I say extra loudly, walking quickly over to the fire and sitting down on one of the logs. Zak's and Lexi's heads spring back like rubber bands and they put enough space between them that Sam could squeeze in the middle. Instead, he joins me on my log. He's wearing some bizarre raccoon hat on his head.

"Where the hell did you go? I was about to call Anna and tell her to send out the rangers to look for you."

"Do not call Anna," I say emphatically. "Or Rachel. They're both busy making out with Keith and Jason." The image makes me feel like bugs are crawling all over my body. "Grossness. Total grossness. I may never be able to look at either of them the same way again."

Lexi laughs. "Those two need to blow off some steam. Let them have some fun for an hour or two. Someday you'll understand."

"Oh, I understand already." I quickly grab a marshmallow from the bag near Sam's feet and stick one on the end of a long twig. "I've been kissed before."

Sam looks at me. "You have?"

"Yeah." I focus on the marshmallow in the fire, watching how it goes from white to a fiery black before burning off and getting crispy. "The kiss was kind of anticlimactic actually. I don't get why everyone's so obsessed with doing it."

"You weren't doing it right," Lexi and Zak say at the same time.

I look up. They're both staring at each other again. Zak looks away first. My face starts to feel hot and then my hands. The fire takes on a bright blue hue, and I know it's happening again. The side effects are about to take over. Maybe it's a good thing, even though it's happening again so quickly. The last thing I want to do right now is watch Lexi and Zak make out while I sit here with Sam.

Lexi shifts uncomfortably on her log and looks at me. "What was so wrong about the kiss?"

"I don't know," I say, reliving when Jack Berger kissed me on that band trip to Phoenix last spring. We had gone for a walk after dinner and were sitting by the hotel pool when it happened. Jack had braces, and I remember feeling them with my lips. It definitely ruined the mood. "It was fine at first, but then he tried to . . ." I can feel his tongue pushing into my mouth. It tasted like Red Hots. I hate Red Hots. "Ick. I don't want to think about it." My speech feels like it's slowing down. I know that's just a side effect of the meds as they kick in. "Kissing is not what it's cracked up to be."

Lexi stands up. "Oh really? You're wrong and I can prove it." She grabs a lantern and runs into the yellow boys' tent. Her body is outlined in black. When she comes back out, she's transformed into a flapper from the Roaring Twenties. Her hair is tucked into a short bob and her bright pink dress is covered in fringe. I know this is just a hallucination, but she looks great as she starts to sing. She sounds a lot like Beyoncé.

"Listen up, honey, learn from me. I'll tell you all about the birds and the bees," Lexi croons, her black gloved hands running up and down her body. "There's boys and men, and nothing between so don't forget to choose very carefully."

I lean in closer, happy to hear my sister bestow some makeout wisdom on me even if I'm imagining this whole thing. Zak is staring at her like I am, though, so maybe this isn't all in my head after all.

"Last guy he went for a grab. His player moves were broken and sad. You'd think he'd be happy with a kiss, nothing nasty, but he ain't getting none from me." Lexi's backup dancers appear at her sides and the three break into a chair dance routine, jumping on and off the chair. "'Cause then he tried to—oh yes—he tried to—oh, what's with all the boys trying to—the bad ones wanna boom ba-ba-boom boom boom. They always wanna boom ba-ba-boom boom boom."

Lexi sits on top of her chair and crosses her long legs as I notice the black garter on her left thigh. Fireworks seem to fall from the sky as she sings. The fireworks are probably just the sparks from the campfire, but the glow around Lexi makes her look larger than life. "When a boy does it right, you won't be able to fight. You'll start to twitch, so scratch that itch. Oh honey, wait for it." She motions for me to join her in the tent.

It looks like so much fun, I can't resist. I jump up and follow her inside and suddenly I'm dressed like a flapper in a hot pink dress similar to my sister's. A feather sticks out of the headband on my head. The two of us sing together. "'Cause then he tried to—oh yes—then he tried to—oh—what's with all the boys trying to? You can't get the boom ba-ba-boom boom until I feel the boom ba-ba-boom boom boom."

When the song ends, I'm actually standing in the tent with Lexi and she's whispering things in my ear about kissing that I never knew before. It sounds like Jack didn't know what he was doing and neither did I. A good kiss should be magical. Maybe the next time a boy kisses me, we can make it a moment worth remembering.

"Whoa!" I hear Sam say from outside the tent. "I don't need to hear that!"

"Either do I," Zak seconds.

Lexi grabs my hand and pulls me back out to the campfire. The two of us are giggling like we used to when we'd have sleepovers. Before she had a life of her own, the two of us were each other's best friend. For a moment, it feels like it once was and maybe it could be that way again. We're still holding hands as we sit back down at the fire.

"Hey." Keith is back.

His hair is messed up and if I'm not mistaken, he's missed a button or two on his shirt. I remember what Lexi said about kissing and smile to myself. Good for Keith.

"What did I miss?" he asks.

The four of us look at each other and try to hide our grins.

"Nothing!" Sam says loudly.

"Nothing at all," Lexi seconds while Zak and I mumble the same.

Keith runs a hand through his hair. "Come on! Why am I always left out? I'm still hip."

Zak groans and we all stand up. This conversation is over.

"Dude, hip?" Zak shakes his head sadly.

Lexi puts a hand on Keith's shoulder. "Calling yourself cool does not make you cool."

"Got it." Keith scratches his head. "I'll have to remember that." He counts heads. "Where's Jason?"

At that moment, my other brother stumbles out of the woods. His hair actually has a twig in it. He raises his hand. "I'm here."

Keith leans over to Jason and examines his neck. "Is that a hickey?"

"Yep!" Jason walks past him.

"You could have lied to me," Keith calls out in the darkness.

Jason just smiles before climbing into the boy tent and collapsing in a heap on his sleeping bag.

Keith sighs. "Let's all get some sleep and figure out where we're going next in the morning."

Sam yawns in agreement and we all turn in. I fall asleep before I can even ask Lexi the one other question I have about kissing—where do I put my hands while the kiss is happening—and the next thing I know the sun is streaming through the tent, birds are chirping loudly like an alarm clock and it's morning. When I venture outside the tent, I already see Sam and Keith sitting at the picnic table in front of the map. Sam has placed twigs and leaves on it marking stops along the California coastline. The campfire from the night before is still smoldering and it looks like someone tried to make oatmeal on the embers for breakfast. I'm not sure it worked. There's also an open box of cereal on the table. Smoke billows up to the sky as an owl hoots in the distance.

"If the campgrounds were flooded, then so were the back roads," Keith surmises as I walk over. His head is covered in a navy sweatshirt hoodie.

Lexi stumbles out behind me. "Then let's stay with the route we're on."

"That's my vote!" Sam seconds.

"No," Jason protests. "The coach at the ball field said the

roads were washed out. Dad would have gone toward the coast. He loved the beach. I say we head west."

"And what?" Lexi asks. "Search the whole Pacific Coast Highway? That's insane."

Everyone starts talking over one another. I pull my red sleeping bag around my shoulders. I forgot how cold it is in the morning at the campgrounds. Zak appears looking sleepy and with bedhead.

"Hold up! I'm in charge," Keith reminds them.

"Unfortunately," Jason mumbles.

Lexi raises her eyebrows at me. I look at the ground. A Hershey's Bar wrapper lies at my feet.

Keith pulls off his hood and looks at Jason. "Do you want to do this? Be in charge? Take care of our finances, figure out Mom's medical bills, and have to leave school to come back here and take care of you guys? That's what you want?" He pushes Jason. "Be my guest!"

"Whoa," Zak says and tries to step in between them.

Jason actually looks apologetic. "You're right. I don't," he says quietly. "I'm sorry."

Keith sighs. "Me too. Let's come up with something that makes sense. Look, Anna said maybe Dad headed someplace fun. A place that made him feel like a kid again."

"Camping is fun," Lexi suggests.

Zak shakes his head. "Camping is *not* fun."

I have an idea. "What about Castle Park? We went every summer and Dad loved it." I pull over the photo box and whip out a picture of us in front of a group of knights in shining armor.

Sam gets excited. "You mean the magical and wondrous Knights of the Round Table Castle Park?"

"It's in the direction we're going." Keith looks at Sam. "Do you like this choice, Navigator?"

"Yes. Let's go for it."

"Okay then, it's settled." Keith looks at Jason who nods. "Let's pack up and move out."

It's easier taking down the tent than putting it up. We pack up the cooler again and throw out our trash. Roll up our sleeping bags and start piling things in the car. Rachel appears suddenly and Jason and she start kissing again. This time it's Lexi who yells out "gross!" I don't say anything. I just jump in the shotgun seat (Sorry, Jason, you snooze, you lose!). I'm putting on my seat belt when Anna appears at Keith's car window. She leans inside and her park ranger hat almost gets caught on the door.

"I'll keep asking around about your dad," Anna tells him. "If I hear anything, I'll call you."

"Call me even if you don't," Keith says, and they kiss through the window.

The backseats break out in applause. Sam whistles.

"All right, all right." I can tell Keith is blushing. "Shut up." We're still giggling when he starts the car. "I'll remember this when it comes to your dating lives."

I smile to myself as Keith pulls down the road again and we pass the sign that says we're leaving Emmet State Park. THANKS FOR VISITING! it says underneath a picture of a friendly cartoon bear. But I'm still thinking about dating. After Lexi's pep talk, I'm actually looking forward to it now.

16 // SAM

Being the youngest in the family usually sucks. Half the time, I'm a ghost. My brothers and sisters like to pretend I'm a figment of their imagination. Keith and Jason never talk about girls in front of me, even though I'm starting to notice them myself. Lexi is a self-absorbed bitch half the time who barely says hello. Whitney is pretty decent most of the time, when she's not popping her meds and staring goofily off into space.

But there are times being the youngest has its advantages and on this road trip I plan on using all of them. Advantage one: When I say I have to pee, I mean I have to pee. Right now. So while Whitney and Keith make small talk, Jason snores in the backseat, Zak stares at Lexi, and Lexi examines her nails, I'm paying attention to the signs along the highway.

HUNGRY? MICKEY'S DINER IS JUST FIFTEEN MILES AHEAD!

That's the diner Harry Freitas said was robbed by a guy that looked like Dad. I focus on the back of Keith's head. He's trying to be all Dad-like on this trip, which means there's no way he'll stop at the diner if he knows what it is. "That's dangerous," Whitney would say. "Are you insane?" Lexi would snap at me.

Dangerous and insane are my middle names on this trip. Go big or go home. Isn't that what Dad always said? And this weekend, I'm going big. We have to find Dad and I'm not going home till we do.

So I pull the little kid card. "Keith? I have to pee."

Whitney groans and Jason shifts in his sleep. He throws one of his bare feet up on the dash and she swats it away.

"Ew, Jason put your socks back on," Whitney moans. "Your feet smell like death and rotten strawberry jam."

"Shut up, I'm trying to sleep," Jason mumbles.

Lexi hits him in the head from the third row. "You're always trying to sleep."

Jason sits up. "Great, you woke me up. Now I've gotta take a leak too. Keith, pull over."

Uh oh. Not what I had planned.

"Aw man!" Whitney groans. "I've got to pee now too."

"Power of the collective mind," Keith says with a sigh. "I have to go now too."

"Me five." Zak raises his hand. "Pull over."

I'm losing control here. "No!" I say a little too loudly and they all look at me. "Can't you guys hold it just a while longer? There's a diner up ahead with flushing toilets."

"What's wrong with the bushes?" Keith asks. "There's a turnoff up ahead."

"That's barbaric." Lexi shudders.

"We were just camping." Keith puts on his turn signal.

"Fifteen measly miles!" I cry out. "Just hold it in."

Keith sighs. "Fine. I guess we can make it."

But when I look out the window again, I see a turquoise pickup truck with a sign painted on its side that says MICKEY'S DINER. I can't risk Jason making Keith pull over before we get to the actual diner. This is our chance. "You know what? It's fine. It's fine. Just pull over right here. I'll go in the bushes."

"Okay." Keith nods while Whitney and Lexi complain.

He pulls up alongside the truck. Smoke is rising from the engine. I can see a guy in a black leather motorcycle jacket and a bandana hovering over the front of the car. A large woman in jeans and a white tee that says MICKEY'S DINER is standing alongside the bumper texting on her phone. While the others scatter into the woods, I hang back. Unfortunately, Keith's Dad-ar is working for a change and he comes back for me.

"Aren't you coming?" he asks.

"I don't have to pee anymore," I lie. I know I'm going to regret this. "I'm good. I'll stay with the car."

Keith looks at me like I'm insane, but he leaves me alone at least. Once he's deep enough into the woods, I walk over to the woman. She's smacking her gum so loud, I can hear it from here.

"Excuse me? Do you work at Mickey's Diner?"

She pulls at her large T-shirt. "That's what it says."

"Okay, I was just wondering, did this man come into the diner Friday night?" I pull a photo of Dad out of my pocket and show it to her to jog her memory.

She adjusts the pink bow in her curly hair and doesn't even look at the picture I'm holding. "I try to block out every single annoying customer that comes into that place."

I'm losing her now too. Why do people always ignore kids? Don't they realize we have important stuff to say too? Well, I'm not being ignored today. "It's my dad," I try again. "He's missing."

Slowly she turns toward me and shoots me that pity look adults always get when I mention my parents. She takes the picture. "Hmm . . . he does kind of look familiar."

My heart starts to thump like Susan's drum in band practice. "Wasn't there a robbery Friday night at the diner? I heard the man got away."

The woman's gum chewing stops and her eyes widen. She looks back at the front of the truck, then begins to gently push me away. "Jesus, kid! Get outta here."

No! She knows something. "Was it him?" I point to the picture again.

She grabs her head and pulls at her bow. "I don't know, kid!" She sounds worked up and nervous. "Could be, maybe. I think the guy was younger." She looks around again and then whispers to me urgently. "The guy took off with most of our cash and Mickey's girlfriend to boot. He'll kill ya if he hears."

She tries to wave me away, but it's too late. From behind her, I see the guy in the navy star-covered bandana move to the back of the truck. It's hard to see his mouth under that long, red scruffy beard, but I can tell he doesn't look happy. Then he grabs a crowbar. "Oh, I heard all right. Let me see that." He motions to my picture. I shove it in my back pocket. "That bastard is your father?"

The waitress steps in between us, but the guy keeps coming at me. "Mickey, calm down."

"I'll kill him!" Mickey roars and lunges for me with the crowbar.

Oh man! I'm dead!

The waitress tries to weave in front of him again. "Run, kid! RUN!"

This time I listen. I run into the woods, my feet snapping twigs and leaves beneath my feet. I stumble over a log, but I keep going. I can hear Mickey screaming not far behind me. Up ahead, Keith is doing his business on a tree.

"Keith! Help! Run! Run!" I shout, waving my arms wildly.

Keith does a double take. "Run? Oh man, run!" He tries to zip up quickly on the go. "Oww! Too tight." He grabs my arm as I pass him and the two of us run deeper into the woods. I'm still yelling when we see Whitney and Lexi. She's crouched down low behind a tree on its side.

"What's going on?" Whitney asks. Her eyes widen when she sees the man with the crowbar. "Oh my God!"

"Run!" Keith and I shout at the same time and they take off with us.

"I can't stop midstream," Lexi complains, pulling up her pants as she lags behind us.

"Get back here!" Mickey shouts, but we're not stupid. We keep going.

Jason and Zak are standing at trees far ahead. They see us coming and jump.

"What the?" Jason starts to say and then sees Mickey. He starts to zip up. "What's going on?"

"No time to explain," I say. "Run!"

"I can't stop midstream!" Zak sounds like Lexi.

"Neither can I," she agrees, pulling him along as he tries to zip up.

Keith stumbles and falls. "Back to the car." He pushes me ahead of him. We run past him and now Keith is bringing up the rear as we head downhill. "Sam!" He sounds out of breath. "Why is there a man with a crowbar chasing us?"

My mouth feels dry as I take deep breaths and try to talk. I can see the car down the hill ahead of us. The waitress is pacing alongside her truck. She sees us and her eyes widen. "He owns the diner Dad robbed."

"That's the diner you wanted to go take a pit stop at?" Keith shouts as he runs ahead and sprints to the car. "That's where you led us?"

"We needed to know!" I argue. Jason blows past all of us and hits the side of the car first.

"Jason!" Keith shouts and throws him the keys. Jason reaches for them and they bounce off his hand and slide under the car.

"Crap! Sorry!" Jason shouts and dives down.

"I'll get them!" I yell and slide under the car. I hit the Unlock button and the car beeps. Above me I hear the others jump in the car. Whitney and Lexi are shrieking. I see Keith's shoes and know he's still out here with me. On the other side of the car are dirty work boots that must belong to Mickey. I lay low and try to crunch myself into a ball so Mickey can't pull me out.

"Calm down." I hear Keith say, out of breath. "I'm sure we can figure this out. It's just a misunderstanding."

"Your dad drive a black Camaro?" Mickey shouts.

"Technically it's dark blue." Keith stumbles over his words.

"He was crying over his depressing life," Mickey says angrily and I see him shuffle around to the other side of the car. Keith moves too so that they're still equally distant. "He needed money real bad. Then he ran off with my blonde, beautiful, but slightly dumb Roxy!" He runs around the car at Keith, and Keith runs to the other side.

"My dad doesn't really cry," Keith pleads. "And he prefers brunettes!"

"Liar!" Mickey taps the crowbar against the truck and I wince.

I see the waitress's sneakers appear. She runs after Mickey and must be trying to hold him back. "Mickey, you're insane!" She shrieks between huffs and puffs. "And I am too out of shape for this nonsense. Just leave the kids alone!"

When they both go around the other side of the truck, I know this is my chance. I grab the keys and slide out from under the car. Then I jump in the front seat.

"Yeah, put down the crowbar," Keith agrees. "I'm a nice guy. I swear!"

"Where's your father?" Mickey growls.

"I'm sorry about this," the waitress says. "He's got anger management issues!"

Keith jumps back. "Ya think?"

"Keith!" I shout and dangle the keys out the window.

Keith sees me and runs to the front passenger seat door. He slides inside. "Go, go, go!" he shouts.

Wait? I get to drive? I start the engine and begin to spin the wheel.

"Keith!" Whitney and Lexi exasperatedly yell at the same time.

"Oh crap!" Keith says and begins to climb over the seat toward me.

Man, I was so close. I see Mickey racing to the car window, and I hit the Lock button. Keith and I quickly slide into our rightful seats as the others in the backseat scream for us to go.

Keith shifts into reverse as Mickey raises the crowbar to hit the dashboard window. We peel out backward, then shift into drive and don't look back. Whitney and Lexi cheer as the dirt plumes behind us.

"Is he coming after us?" Keith asks, sounding anxious.

I look back. Mickey and the waitress are just standing there. Mickey is jumping up and down but his figure gets smaller and smaller the farther we get away. "Nope, we're safe."

"What were you thinking?" Lexi yells at me, but ruffles my hair so I know she's not too ticked. "You could have gotten us killed!"

I puff up my chest. "I'd like to see them try to mess with us."

"Can you believe that crazy guy?" Whitney adds. "There's no way Dad would go for some twenty-year-old bimbo."

Lexi's face scrunches up. "That's disgusting." Everyone agrees.

Keith is the only one who's quiet. I look over and his eyes are on the highway stretched out in front of us. "No way. Not our dad," he whispers. He speeds up slightly, and I'm envious. I was this close to getting to drive today! "From here on out, no more bathroom breaks."

I wince. "Um . . ."

Keith does a double take. "What? You've got to be kidding me!"

"I get a nervous bladder in high-stress situations," I say.

"Just hold it!" Everyone in the car yells and I cover my head before they can throw stuff.

"We can't be too far from Castle Park now anyway." Lexi peers out the window. "You can go there."

Whitney points as trees and bushes fly by. A big green sign shows the turnoff for the park is just fifteen miles down the road. "That's it!"

"Oh thank God," I say and readjust my position slightly so I can hold it in till we get there. I don't talk till we're pulling off the highway and into the Castle parking lot. Now I'm so excited, I pee on a flower box near the picnic table area. I can't help it. I was never going to make it across the moat to the ticket booth.

"Gross, Sam!" Lexi tells me.

Too bad. I can't wait another minute to get in the park.

The lot is empty when we arrive, which is weird because a theme park should be open by noon, shouldn't it? Maybe it's got shorter hours in the spring. I run up ahead of Lexi and the others now that I've finished my business. The castle looms up ahead. I bet the place looks exactly like it did when we were last here. Dad said they hadn't updated any of the rides since he was a teenager. Castle Park has a boat flume with a dragon that stares at you from a cave, cable cars that go the length of the park, a huge slide you can ride down in potato sacks, and my ultimate favorite—the Knights of the Round Table show where knights duel one another on horses. Each side of the arena gets to pick a knight to root for. Somehow the side Dad and I always picked won. He loved that show as much as I did. I'm not going to say this to the others because they'll just make fun of me, but maybe Dad is actually working here now as a knight in the show? If Keith's right about Dad wanting to be a kid again, there's no place better to do that than Castle Park. If they still have the show. I'm so making Keith stay for it, so I can search for Dad. If he's not there, then at least I get to see the knights again. And maybe go on that boat ride.

After my quick pee stop along the fence line, we're racing each other up the path to the castle, which looks exactly how I remembered it.

"It's the magical, wondrous Knights of the Round Table Castle Park!" I shout. I know I sound like I'm five, but I don't care. This place is awesome! It's huge, white, and covered in leafy vines, but with signs directing you to the knight minigolf course on the left and the park entrance on the right. No matter what we're doing first, Dad knew I always liked to go through the castle—which is really just a big gift show—first so that I got to feel like a real knight.

But today when I reach the castle first, I see it's locked up tight with a chain.

CLOSED! SEE YOU NEXT SEASON! reads a sign on the doors.

I just stand there and stare at it like it's a mirage. I can feel my heart beating against my chest.

"How can they be closed?" Whitney asks, looking as dumb-founded as I am.

Lexi frowns and puts her arm around me, which is weird. She rarely acts big sisterly. Then she starts rubbing my back. Who stole my mean sister? "We only used to come here during the summer," she says apologetically. "I guess it's too early in the season for it to be open now."

Zak and Jason don't take that reasoning as an answer. Both of them start to scale the castle gates that line either side of the moat. Jason grabs a vine and tries to pull himself high enough to see over the castle wall.

"The place is totally shut down," he tells us as he peeks over the other side. I feel jealous that he gets to see in and I don't. "We could totally sneak in, though. I don't see any guards."

"Why would we do that?" I blurt out, feeling suddenly cranky. "Dad's obviously not here."

"So this is just another dead end?" Lexi asks, her voice wavering.

"We should head back." I hear Keith say and then he turns around. He's staring at all of us, his hands in his pockets, looking like there's a lot more he wants to say, but isn't going to.

"No! There's tons of other pictures to follow," I insist. Behind me, I hear Zak and Jason jump off the wall and walk over.

"Sam's right. We've barely started," Whitney agrees with me. "We can't head back now."

Keith shifts uncomfortably. "What we have to do is get you all back for school tomorrow."

"No," Whitney moans. "It's only school."

"Maybe for you, but Jason and Lexi are an inch away from flunking out. I can't add that to our problems right now," Keith reminds us.

"So take them back," I snap. "I'm not giving up."

"Sam, look." Keith puts an arm around me too. Suddenly the Connollys are all affectionate again? "We've hit every place Dad would have stopped on this route, right?"

"I guess." I stare at the ground, which looks like a cobble-stone path.

"We'll try again next weekend and go in another direction with new photos," Keith suggests.

"You promise?" Lexi asks.

"I promise." Keith crosses his heart. "Besides, it's not like I could stop you guys even if I wanted to."

We sort of laugh. Emphasis on the sort of.

"I want to find him too," Keith insists and I believe him.

"Next weekend," Jason agrees and we all start heading back to the car.

I look back at the castle one more time and try to remember the stone pattern, the turrets, the vines creeping up the stained-glass windows. I do what my art teacher says to do all the time: commit a place to memory. Yes, I want to draw the castle later, but I also have another reason for taking a walk down memory lane. And it's a bummer.

I'm pretty sure I'll never see this place again, not without Dad around to take me.

17 // WHITNEY

I forgot what a long drive home it is from Castle Park. We stopped to eat at a McDonald's—Keith thought it was the only place safe enough for us to assume no one had seen Dad (he hates fast food). By the time we get home, it's nighttime and we're all exhausted. Zak takes off for his house, and the rest of us walk up the path together. Lexi is talking to me about this thrift store she's become obsessed with and says I need to try, which is sort of amazing because the other night she made it sound like my fashion taste was too hopeless to be helped. We're both so busy debating skinny jeans and jeggings that we open the door and totally miss the sign on it.

"What is that?" Jason asks and I turn around to see Keith tapping a piece of paper on the front door.

I feel the chicken nuggets I had at dinner start to come back up.

EVICTION NOTICE the paper says in large, black block letters.

Keith rips it down and reads the small print underneath. "It's a foreclosure notice."

"Already?" Sam freaks out.

Keith is just staring at the paper. "I guess so," he responds quietly.

We all start talking at once. Lexi, who was halfway up the stairs comes racing back down.

"When do we have to leave?" Sam asks despondently.

"What are we going to do?" Lexi wants to know, her voice rising.

"I don't know." Keith's voice cracks.

"What do you mean you don't know?" Jason is starting to Hulk out again.

"We're going to have to live on the streets," Sam freaks out. "We're homeless!"

The thought dawns on Lexi and she starts to hyperventilate. "Oh my God, we're homeless now?" She races halfway up the stairs again and stares longingly at the old family portraits that hang on the wall.

I feel the world start to spin. My eyes begin to glaze over. I took my nighttime dose of my medication back when we were in the car, but nothing happened. Now I know why—I wasn't upset for a change. Fifteen minutes ago, my family was semi-normal again. We'd had a weekend away together and survived. We were laughing in the car about Jason's foot stench, Keith's makeout session in the woods, Lexi's sex talk at the campfire, and Sam almost getting us all killed by that crazy dude with the crowbar. It was just the five of us (well, and Zak) having a decent time together. I can't remember the last time we were so in sync. What started out as a Dad mission had turned into something much more—a chance to find our way back to each other. But now, all of us are standing in the foyer, which is littered with week-old newspapers, and we're arguing again.

Welcome home, Connollys.

But not for long.

Keith is still staring at the eviction notice like it has all the answers to our problems on it. I feel like I need to shake him. He's in charge till we find Dad. He has to know what to do next. He has to have a plan. "Keith, we're broke." I'm trying to bring him back to us. "Really broke. How are we going to pay for gas and clothes and food?" He's still not saying anything. "Keith!" I yell, trying to get through to him.

And that's when he completely snaps. "I don't know, okay? I don't know!" He runs a hand through his dark brown hair. "Jesus, I'm barely old enough to take care of myself."

Lexi runs back downstairs again when she hears Keith screaming.

I've never heard him this unhinged. He starts to walk away, but I can't let him. Not without knowing where we go from here. "Keith, what about Dad. Maybe—"

He spins around. "Dad left us!" he shouts in my face. "Dad abandoned us!" He turns to each of us. "Get that through your heads! All of you! He left us and he's not coming back!" He crumples up the eviction notice into a ball. "We're screwed." He throws it on the ground and barrels up the stairs.

Everyone scatters and I just stand there in the doorway, realizing the door is still wide open. I wonder if any of the neighbors heard the outburst. Have they seen the eviction notice? Have the She-Bitches passed and taken pictures of it and put them on CHAT MUCH? My breathing becomes labored. I close the door and lean against it, unsure of what to do. The foyer continues to spin and becomes grainy. I feel like I'm watching an old home movie that jumps and skips and has black lines running through it. The film is washed in blue tones.

I should check on Keith. I run up the stairs and see him down the hall in our parents' room. He's trashing the place. His hand runs across their mahogany desk, then he pulls open the drawers, searching for something. Next he overturns the bedding and pillows, pulls clothes out of the closet, and then finally pulls out a firebox. For a moment, he seems relieved, till he opens it, and it's just filled with more papers that have no answers. When he hurls it across the room, I scatter.

I pass Jason's room where he's FaceTiming with Zak.

"Coach e-mailed me while we were away." I hear Jason tell him. His voice is monotone and hoarse. "I'm off the team. He told the scout from UCLA not to bother coming."

"You have to talk to him!" Zak insists. "Get him to take you back. It's only your junior year, dude. You can still—"

Jason slams his laptop closed, ending the conversation. I watch him pick up a baseball bat and I inhale sharply. *BOOM!* He takes it to his trophy shelf and begins batting them off the shelves. One hits his window and cracks.

"Who cares?" He says to no one. I hide behind the door in the hallway so he can't see me. "We can't afford to live here anyway! Why would I be able to afford college?" I hear the baseball bat drop with a *thud*. "None of this matters anymore."

Lexi walks past me without making eye contact. She's reapplied the dark liner and smoky eye shadows that were missing the last two days and now she's wearing a black dress that's so tight it looks like panty hose. It barely covers her butt.

"Where are you going?" I ask, feeling weak in the knees when I look out the window. Sam is in the backyard. I watch him dump his art supplies and easel into a trash can. "Don't leave right now," I beg. "Everything's going to hell." I grab her arm and she shrugs me off. I watch her take a swig of who-knows-what from the tiny flask she usually keeps hidden in her dresser drawer.

"Whit, it's always been hell here, didn't you know?" Lexi's words are slurring slightly. She stumbles to the staircase and drops her phone. I pick it up and see the text.

JARED CELL: Party. Come on.

"Don't go!" I yell to her and she turns around. I'm desperate. She looks like the old Lexi again, the one who's blessedly been absent this weekend. I don't like this Lexi. I want the original back. "I'll tell Keith," I threaten.

She rolls her eyes and heads back to her room. "There's other ways to get out of here, you know."

But for the moment, I'm relieved. Lexi's phone vibrates in my hands.

ZAK CELL: Check on Jason. Is he OK? Off team.

I hear Jason smashing more trophies and Lexi crying in her room. I don't know what to do. The sky is dark; the hallway is in deep shades of blue. I'm not sure how much longer I can hold on. I text Zak back in caps.

IT'S WHIT. HAVE LEXI'S PHONE. NEED HELP HERE. EVERYONE FREAKING OUT. WE'RE BEING EVICTED!!!

Zak's reply is almost instant.

ZAK CELL: I'm on my way. Hang on!

I'm not sure I can hang on. My world is crumbling, and I'm fading away from reality again.

"Who am I?" Jason seems to sing angrily, as he continues to pull apart all memories of his baseball career. "What am I? Tell me now. Just break it all away. Take it all away!"

I walk down the hall and find Keith sitting in Mom and Dad's closet. He pulls clothes off hangers as he shouts out the words. "I'm sitting here in pieces of fractured fears so tear it down. Tear it down! I want to tear it down!"

I whirl around. There's nowhere else to go. They're all around me and they seem to be in worse shape than I am for once. I'm just scared. They're maniacal and destructive and I'm worried by the time Zak gets here, the whole house could crumble down around us.

"Tear me down! Tear me down!" Lexi, Jason, and Keith sing like they're in a trance.

It's Lexi I'm most worried about. She's always been the most self-destructive. I race back to her room and see her standing in front of her bedroom window, staring out at the moon. Her flask is in her hand.

"Standing on the edge," she sings quietly and I see her move to open the window. "This window's open again. I am nothing, nothing left."

No good. Where is Zak? I need help here! I run back down the hall. Keith is the only one who can stop her. He's off the floor at least, but he's still moving like a zombie. I spin him toward me and shake him. His eyes light up with recognition.

"I know we're almost spent, nothing left, can't pay the rent!

I'm not giving up yet!" I sing to him and put my arm out. "Take my hand. Hold it out. I will pull you in."

"It's Lexi," I say, breathing fast, and forgetting the song for a moment. "Jason too. We need you." Keith doesn't need to know more. He kicks into high gear and takes my hand. We race down the hall. He goes straight to Lexi's room while I stop first at Jason's. For once, I'm worried he could really hurt himself.

"What am I doing with this?" Jason sings to the bat in his hand. All of his trophies lie in pieces on the floor. From Little League to the high school state championship. Broken and beaten, just like Jason. "I'd rather it break and twist," he sings, sounding hollow. I try to wrestle the bat away from him before he hurts himself. Jason's too strong for me and the two of us are engaged in a tug of war. I'm losing miserably. Then I see another hand grab the bat above mine. Zak! He pulls harder and whips the bat away from Jason. Jason just stands there, seemingly defeated, and I remember we still have Lexi to worry about.

I leave Zak with Jason and run to the next room where Keith is trying to coax my sister off the window ledge. With one hand, he yanks Lexi down and with the other he grabs her flask.

"No!" she screams and starts to hit him, but Keith keeps walking toward the bathroom Lexi shares with Jason, side-stepping clothes and shoes and dirty laundry, to pour the vodka down the sink. Lexi is hitting him hard. Tears stream down her face, but Keith ignores her and continues to let the liquid wash away. The stench of alcohol burns my nose and my stomach aches. Finally, Lexi stops hitting him and stands there defeated, just like Jason.

He appears in the bathroom doorway as Zak lingers behind.

"Tear me down, please pull me back," Jason and Lexi sing. "Pull me back."

"I know we're almost spent," Keith and I sing to them. I grab Lexi's hand. Keith puts one on Jason's shoulder. "Nothing left, can't pay the rent." It sounds bad, I know, but Keith and I look at each other and realize we're not ready to fall apart. "I'm not giving up yet!" we sing together.

With an arm around both of them, Keith and I lead Jason and Lexi downstairs. They're quiet, but calm and there's still one Connolly left to wrestle with. I look back at Zak and mouth "thank you." He waves me away, knowing this is a family moment. Wordlessly, I lead the others outside to the backyard where I last saw Sam.

We're just in time to see my little brother light a match and prepare to torch all of his artwork in the trash can. I pull away from the others and make it to Sam in time to blow the match out.

"Let's not go so far," I sing softly. "Up in flames and scars."

Sam just hangs his head as I pull some of his drawings out of the trash. I hand the others Sam's sketchpad with the picture of the meadow and one of a tiger in it. The others gather around and flip through the pad. Lexi pulls some more drawings out of the trash. They look as amazed as I am that there's an artist in the family. I look at Sam. He actually looks relieved to be caught and I can't blame him. He's been out in the cold for so long—we all have really—and if Dad really has skipped town on us and is never coming back—then all we have is each other. We worked well this weekend. Is there any reason to believe we can't survive whatever is thrown at us now as long as we stick together? I pull him into a hug.

"I think it's time to sleep," I sing to the others. "Let this nightmare end and turn into a dream. I know we're almost spent. Nothing left. I'm not giving up yet." I put my hand out and wait for the others to pile on top of mine like we're the team I know we can be. "Take my hand, hold it out. I will pull you in."

Slowly the others put their hands in. We all look at each other and I see the grainy blue of the movie in my head start to fade away again. I concentrate on Keith's dark brown eyes, which are focused on my own, and then I look at Lexi's sad ones. She stares at Jason and he stares at Sam. I don't need a hallucination when I have them to back me up. This is it. As good as it's going to get from here on out. If Keith is right and Dad isn't coming back, all we have is this group of people right here. Life might suck from here on out, but we have to stick together.

Keith must be thinking the same thing because he grips my hand tighter and then someone pulls us all in for a tight hug. We just stand there and listen to the sounds of the night. Crickets singing their song, a lone car alarm going off in the distance, a plane flying overhead. I concentrate on the sound of our breathing. It was so labored a few moments ago, but now it's slowing back down to a normal pace. *Normal.* Lexi moves closer to me. Jason leans into Keith who is holding Sam tight. Keith and I smile at each other.

Our lives may never be what they once were, but maybe there's a way we can create a new normal together.

18 // KEITH

Shit happens.

I'd like to patent that phrase on a car bumper sticker to make some cash, but I think someone already beat me to it. Doesn't matter—it's still the new Connolly family slogan.

When we walked in last night and I saw the eviction notice on the front door, I felt like I was in the middle of a major California earthquake. The ground was moving, the walls were shaking, and the screaming—mostly from me—was so loud it could shatter windows.

My first thought when I saw that paper: we're screwed.

Lexi, Jason, Whitney, and even Sam knew it too. Where were we going to live? How would we get money? How the hell was I going to provide for this family I've suddenly become the sole parent of? It's a sucky position to be in, and I could continue to whine about it and get pissed off at Mom for dying, Dad for bailing, Harry for not giving me an escape plan and the world for turning against us, but you know what? It wouldn't change a damn thing.

Shit happens and you just have to deal with it.

Last night, that's exactly what each of us did in our own way, I guess. Jason caused his own earthquake in his room and destroyed every trophy he's ever won. Sam tried to torch his artwork. Lexi literally tried to go over the edge and Whitney, well, she was the glue that held us together, now that I think about it. She's already had her meltdowns. Now it was our turn.

So we did. We melted down. We screamed. We cried, and we friggin' held each other too. We stood out in the backyard that would soon belong to a new family and we just hung on to each other for dear life till it didn't hurt so much anymore. Hell, it's always going to hurt, but we've got to move past it and stop crying over things we can't control. If Dad wants to abandon us, then screw Dad. We don't need him. We've got one another and this morning, we're moving on the only way we can.

Sam and I took down a bunch of old school photos and used the frames to mount his artwork for the fair. I've made it a mandatory order that we all attend his show tomorrow—not that anyone was going to fight me. Lexi hasn't shut up about what Sam's going to wear. Hell, Jason even made everyone waffles to celebrate Sam's accomplishment. Whitney hasn't been able to wipe the goofy grin off her face all morning.

There's a knock at the side door in the kitchen and seconds later Whitney's best friend, Susan, walks in. "Whit, get out of bed—oh!" She sees us all around the island (which is decluttered and Windexed for a change, thank you very much), eating breakfast, dressed, and ready to start the day and the girl nearly passes out.

I guess we have been kind of a mess the last few months.

"What happened here?" Susan's eyes bulge out of her head when she sees Jason at the stove with a spatula. "Jason's cooking?"

"Yep!" He lifts the frying pan and flips a waffle in midair. "Want some breakfast?"

Susan looks from Whitney to me and I nod. "Um, sure." She pulls out a stool and sits down at the island.

I pull one of Sam's paintings out of the way. "The glue's still wet on this one, so let me move it. Sam's been chosen as a finalist for the county art show," I say proudly and Sam's smile is so bright, it has enough wattage to light the entire house.

Susan turns to him. "That's awesome!"

"Thanks," Sam mumbles in between bites of waffle. He stops chewing when he sees Lexi.

I turn to see what he's staring at and I almost fall off my stool. Lexi's traded in her hard rocker look for a preppy pastel dress and sweater. Her hair is straightened and her makeup is really pretty and normal. No raccoon eyes. She carries her backpack over to the kitchen buffet and begins putting her textbooks in it.

"Are you putting books in your backpack?" Susan asks, reading my thoughts.

"Yep." Lexi zips up the bag. She looks at me. "I'm going to need books if I'm going to class and actually plan on passing this semester." I give her a thumbs-up.

Jason places a plate of steaming waffles in front of Susan, and Sam pours her a glass of orange juice. Whitney hands her a napkin and fork, and Susan bangs her hands on the island. "Okay, what happened on this road trip of yours? Did you all get possessed or something?"

Zak walks in the kitchen and takes a waffle off the stack in the middle of the table. "There was kind of an exorcism last night. Be glad you missed it." He does a double take when he sees Lexi's outfit, but doesn't say anything.

"Do you guys want a ride to school?" Lexi asks Susan and Whitney.

The girls look at each other. "Wait, really? Like in the same car as you?"

"YES!" Susan blurts out. She leans closer to Lexi. Her eyes are sort of wild. "We'll definitely ride with you. Can you take us home later as well?"

"Why?" Whitney sounds nervous. "What's going on now?"

"Well," Susan drags the word out and adjusts her glasses on her nose. "The She-Bitches had a field day with you not being at the car wash. They said you were being a cry baby and were hiding from them."

"She-Bitches?" I ask, getting worried. I've been so consumed with keeping the house safe that I forgot I also had my siblings to protect. What else has been going on under my nose in this house that I've missed? "Who are the She-Bitches?"

Susan looks at Whitney quickly and frowns. "Melanie and her bitchy friends, hence the She-Bitch nickname. They don't know we call them that," she adds quickly.

Whitney pulls her phone out of her jeans pocket. When she looks at the screen, she groans. "CHAT MUCH? has a whole feed on me. Today is going to be rough."

"Wait? These She-Bitches are starting with you on CHAT MUCH?" Lexi pulls the phone out of Whitney's hand and I look at the screen with her. There's a bunch of comments about Whitney on there that make my skin burn. What is with high school girls?

"It's fine, really," Whitney says quickly and tries to take her phone back.

"No, it's not fine," I say. "Who the hell do these girls think they are calling you this stuff? I'm going to call the principal."

Susan and Whitney moan. "They'll call me a narc!" Whitney panics. "You'll just make things worse."

"They already make our lives a living hell," Susan adds

and munches on a waffle. "They'll bury us if you tell the school what's going on."

"How can we make things worse? These bitches are talking crap about you for no reason!" Lexi snaps.

Jason walks over from the stove and looks at Whitney's phone. He taps the screen. "I know that girl. She's the stuck-up sophomore in my government class."

"Why didn't you tell us what these girls were doing?" I ask, feeling awful.

Whitney's cheeks flush. She grabs Susan's arm and pulls her away from the table. "Because it's embarrassing, okay?" Whitney throws her bag over her shoulder. "Come on, we'll be late for school." She walks out the side door ahead of Jason and Lexi.

Lexi looks at him. "We are so taking those bitches down."

"Hell, yeah!" Jason agrees and grabs his bag. "I'm ready to kick some ass."

"Thank God," Susan says and breathes a sigh of relief as she places her backpack over her shoulders. "We need allies." She heads out the door with Lexi.

I put my hand on Jason's shoulder and hold him back. "I'll meet you after school and we'll talk to your coach together."

Jason's face freezes and I notice it's the first time in a long time I've seen him look vulnerable instead of like the Hulk. I know he misses playing ball even if he says the opposite. "Are you sure this will work?"

"We'll grovel and beg and you'll promise to be on your best behavior," I instruct him. "And we'll work on getting that scout back to see you."

"But college is out of our league right now. It's too expensive."

"Hence, working on getting you an athletic scholarship," I say and Jason's eyes widen with recognition. Yeah, he didn't think of that card, did he? He gives me a rare smile and I steer him to the door along with Sam. "I'll see you guys later!"

I shut the door behind them and the house is quiet. The hum of the fridge is the only sound along with that annoyingly loud ice machine in it. I look around and try to think of where to start first. Mom's china is the first thing that comes to mind. I head to the dining room and open the cabinet where her china and crystal are on display. I've already gathered a bunch of boxes to pack things up in. It's time I dig in and sell some of this stuff so I can make a life for this family again.

I run my hand along the edge of the antique mahogany table, where today's paper sits opened to the classified section. I've already circled a number of jobs I'm going to call about. I've even found some decent apartment listings in the area that we might be able to afford if I get a job. I've got a lot to do and not a lot of time to do it. Wandering into the living room, I pass the furniture that can definitely be sold since they're antiques and I stop when I see the piano.

Parting with this baby is going to be the toughest. We took lessons on this piano that once belonged to my grandparents. It's a Steinway, for God's sake, and it's in mint condition. It should bring in some nice dough, but it kills me to think of it in someone else's home. It kills me to think of any of our things in someone else's home.

Shit, I'm such a girl thinking this crap. I'm glad Jason isn't here to see me get all misty.

I look around the living room where we celebrated so many Christmases, birthdays, communions, and milestones. I have to remember where we live may change, but our memories don't have to. I grab a white sheet from the pile on the couch and slowly cover this beauty up, saying a quick prayer that the person who takes this piano home has kids who will get to enjoy it as much as I did.

Okay, sappy memory lane time is over.

Shit happens. Back to job hunting and getting on with life as it is now.

19 //
WHITNEY

Jason drove us to school. Coming home, I insist on walking.

Susan thinks I've officially lost it.

She's running bush to bush along our usual path. "Tell me again why we didn't ride with Lexi?"

I hold my head high and keep looking straight ahead. "I need to face this on my own."

Susan runs to a tree and hides behind it. "What? Your imminent death?"

I stop and look at her. "I'm not afraid of them anymore," I say evenly.

"Why? Did you find God and see Jesus on your road trip?"

"No. I just realized that if I can handle all the crap that's been thrown at my family, and what's happened with my parents, then I can certainly handle Melanie and those two vapid Barbies she calls her friends." Wow, just saying that out loud makes me feel like a superhero. Maybe I'm not going to hallucinate when I see the She-Bitches. Could it be, I finally have these side effects under control?

I hear Susan squeak. I look down the road and see the familiar yellow convertible cruising down our block, ready to wage war. "Okay, well, now's your chance," she says in a panicky voice as she hovers behind a tree branch.

I imagine Jason and I are watching *The Avengers*. We already call him Hulk. Maybe I'm Black Widow. This is my moment to dominate. I stand my ground and wave as their Mini Coop grinds to a halt in front of us. "Hello, ladies!"

Melanie removes her red sunglasses and her bottle-blonde hair seems to fall in ripples around her heart-shaped face. Her eyes narrow at me and she adjusts her blue paisley top. She looks at her redheaded peeps, who jump up on their seats like they usually do when they slow down their car to insult Susan and me. Melanie's sucking on a lollipop. She pulls it out of her mouth and lets it dangle in her fingers. "Is she talking to us?" She shoots me a nasty smile. "Or just crying to her skanky big sister." The other girls high-five like monkeys. All the other two do is mimic.

Susan is still hiding, but I'm not giving up this fight today. I may have lost my parents. I may have lost my house. I'll be damned if I continue to let these bitches take away my dignity. "You're right. I shouldn't waste my time talking to you losers."

They stop laughing. "What did you just call us?"

"Go away, Melanie," I say firmly. "I'm done." I point to Susan and me. "We're done. Say what you want about me from here on out. I don't care. I'm not listening." I throw up my hands. "You can write nasty things on CHAT MUCH? and guess what? From here on out, I'll write back." Melanie shifts uncomfortably in the driver's seat. I move closer to the car and lean over the rolled down windows. "I already know I'm smarter than you—after all, you cheat on me in class—so when I make a dig at you, they'll be way more clever than yours ever were."

"Wow." I hear Susan whisper as she finally emerges from behind her tree branch.

Melanie pulls herself out of her seat and gets in my face. "How dare you!"

I feel my body flinch slightly and then the world's sounds seem to amplify. The lawnmower next door sounds louder. The birds chirp at a high octave, and the blue sky is washed away in a rainbow of colors. I guess I still need my hallucinations to deal with a girl like Melanie, but you know what? Who cares if I do? Side effects or not, I'm tackling this bully head on for a change. I let the world shift colors and my jeans and flannel transform into a superhero costume, but I don't back down. "Go ahead. Touch me. Throw eggs at us," I say calmly and play with the new badass black leather gloves I seem to have on. "I'll have you arrested for assault."

When I back away from the car, I'm wearing a red spandex pantsuit. I hear music start to play in my head. It's Susan's and my favorite song—"Roar" by Katy Perry—and it has all the girl power I need to make it through this long-overdue confrontation with the She-Bitches. Dark storm clouds seem to fill the sky as Susan transforms into her own ensemble. Sam pops up out of nowhere in an orange jumpsuit, cape, and a mask. Jason is next in a yellow superhero outfit that has a baseball symbol on his chest. I'm not sure if I'm imagining this, but Lexi pulls up in her car in a hot pink spandex number. Her mask is beautifully adorned like she's headed to a masquerade ball. Susan has on the lavender version of the same outfit. The three of them give a kick in unison and then a series of punches. Cartoonish bubbles appear above their heads like in a comic book. POW! WHAM! ZAP! they read.

The She-Bitches are suddenly out of the Mini Coop and in their own villainous getups. Coordinating Technicolor dresses, of course, with black gloves, masks, and headbands that make them look like devils. But I'm not scared of them. Not anymore.

I sing the song at the top of my lungs. I know every word, but I've never really meant it before now. Looking at Melanie and her vapid friends in their getups. I almost feel sorry for them. All they have is their nastiness. I may have lost a lot, but I still have my family and I have a real best friend who won't take crap behind my back. Melanie probably doesn't know what a real friend is, and if she continues to treat people the way she does, she never will.

I roar in Melanie's face about being a champion while Susan and Lexi back me up and the girl seems terrified.

Just as quickly, my hallucination fades, and my flannel shirt and maroon jeans are back. Susan has on that cute tie-dyed tank top again. The only thing different now is Lexi is actually here. She really did pull up in her car. The three of us stand united and stare down the girls.

"Did you hear what I just said?" I repeat. "You can't hurt me or Susan anymore. Go spend money at the mall or something."

"But don't come back here," Lexi threatens them. I hear a door open and turn around. Keith and Sam and are walking across the lawn toward Melanie's car. She sees them and her face whitens.

"'Cause if you come back here ever again, or bother Susan and me in school, I will take you down," I finish, feeling pretty pleased with myself. "That's a promise."

Melanie slides her sunglasses back over her eyes. If I'm not mistaken, her hands are shaking. The other wannabes slide into their seats without a word and look down at their feet.

"Whatever," Melanie says meekly. She quickly starts her car and drives away.

I wait till the yellow Mini Coop is almost out of sight before I let myself get excited.

I did it. I faced the She-Bitches, and I WON. Holy crap!

I scream loudly and start jumping up and down. Susan grabs my hands and jumps with me as Lexi laughs at us. Then I grab her hand and she starts jumping too. Sam can't resist and soon he's strumming an air guitar. Keith lets loose and pretends to drum.

We must look pretty silly out here on the lawn, but for the first time in a long time, I don't care what anybody thinks of me or my family.

I'm a fighter and I'm finally ready for the world to hear me roar.

20 // JASON

Goddamn it, Keith. Your master plan worked. I'm back on the team, and hell, it feels good. I didn't think it would after spending so much time hating the game, hating the coach, hating my friggin' arm that has sucked so bad this season, but I don't know. Something major happened last night to all of us—we finally took a step forward.

I didn't cry—it's not my style—but taking a bat to my trophies unlocked something deep inside me that I needed to let go of: my anger. Sam and Whitney are right to call me the Hulk. You won't like me when I'm angry. I haven't liked myself much the last few months either. Who knew it was so tiring to be pissed off all the time? Unleash the fury and clear your head. That's what I did and it helped. My arm is a little rusty, but it's working again. I struck out six guys in practice this afternoon, and I know they weren't going easy on me either. Some of the team is kind of pissed about how I bailed on them this season. I get it. I'm pissed at me too.

But I'm back, baby, and I'm not going anywhere ever again.

I pack up my bag in the dugout and head out when I run into Zak, who's waiting for me by our cars.

"So you're officially back on the team?" he asks hopefully.

"I'm on probation," I stress, and hike my baseball bag higher on my right shoulder. "Coach reamed me out good. Said I pretty much had to pitch a no-hitter to start again, but Keith talked to him too and I think he'll come around. I kicked ass in practice today. I just have to keep it up. Want to hit the cages tonight?"

"I'll take pity on you and help you out."

I nudge Zak and practically knock him into my car. He throws his bag into the backseat and I do the same. The two of us climb in. Guess I should throw him a bone since he agreed to throw me one. "So what's up with you and my sister?"

Zak looks at me incredulously as he slides on his seat belt. "Now you ask?"

"She's been acting weird—you saw what she was wearing today—and it's freaking me out," I say and turn the car key. "She's old Lexi again."

"Maybe," Zak says quietly. "I'd pretty much given up on her."

Crap, he really likes her. Look how pathetic his face is right now. "Make her jealous," I blurt out.

"What?"

"She's super competitive and equally stubborn. You'll have to force her to admit her feelings if you want a shot."

Zak's face brightens. Man, am I going to tease him about this later. "You think she has feelings for me?"

I fake gag. "Yeah, I can't do this. I tried. You and my sister . . ."

I shutter. "This is as far as I can go with this conversation without officially throwing up."

Zak puts a hand on mine. "You mean you don't want to let me braid your hair while we talk about your feelings now?"

I pull my hand away. "Bite me."

When we pull up at my house—which let's face it, is kind of Zak's as well at this point—I see those She-Bitches, or whatever Whitney calls them, peeling away and my family with Susan on the front steps.

Zak lowers his aviator shades. "What they hell are they doing?"

"Having some sort of dance party . . . on the front lawn," I say as dumbfounded as he is. We don't bother pulling all the way up the driveway to the back. We just stop in front and get out to see what's happening. Keith is spinning Lexi around like a ballerina, and Susan and Whitney have formed a Sam sandwich. "Have you guys lost your minds?" I ask. I side-eye a nanny walking past with a double stroller. She looks at us like we're nuts. "Families with eviction notices on their front door don't usually look this happy."

Lexi puts her arm around Whitney. "Whit here stood up to the She-Bitches."

"With their help." Whitney smiles ear to ear.

"I don't think they're going to bother us anymore," Susan adds like she can't believe it. "We can walk down the halls now without anyone taping notes to our back or spiking our Sprites with Visine!"

"Visine in Sprite," Sam repeats. "What does that do?"

Keith gives Sam a head noogie. "Never mind!"

"Seems like we should celebrate Whit's victory or something," I suggest and give my sister a high five.

She smiles. "We have to celebrate you too, you know. We heard you're back on the team."

I look at Keith. He looks proud of me for a change. I'll never admit this, but it's a hell of a good feeling. "I'm on probation, but yeah, I'm on the team."

Sam whistles and Susan applauds. I take a mock bow. Then I take Whitney's hand and she bows. Then the two of us bow together. Shit, we look corny. The nanny walking by hurries away. She's probably off to tell her employers how weird the Connollys are. Who the hell cares? We're only here another week.

"How about a game of ball in the backyard?" Sam suggests excitedly. "Boys versus girls?"

Zak scratches his chin. "I like those odds. You're on, right, boys?"

Keith and I nod. "I'm in," I say trying to be easygoing for a change.

I've been a royal ass lately so being agreeable is not going to come easy. But if Lexi can stop dressing like a streetwalker, I can try not to Hulk out all the time.

It only takes us a few minutes to move some furniture so that we have enough room for a proper ball field. Whitney and Susan grab some empty pizza boxes from the trash to use as bases. I try not to look at the garbage by the side of the house. Looks like Keith has had the unwelcome task today of starting to clear the decks around here.

"Hey, batter, batter!" Sam pounds his mitt with his fist while he jumps up and down by second base. He's trying to spook Susan who's up at bat first. It's working.

"Sam, cut it out," Whitney complains. "Go for it, S!"

"I got this!" Susan says and takes a few poor practice swings. "I got this!"

I almost feel bad pitching to the girl, but it's nice to be on the mound, so to speak, again. I wind up and throw her a fastball. The ball comes dangerously close to striking her and she misses it.

"Whoa!"

Zak catches the ball when it flies past her. He's balancing on his knees with a catcher's mask on his face. "Strike one!" I hear his muffled voice cry.

"You can't hit a girl." Susan gives me the stink eye.

I catch the ball when Zak rockets it back. "I didn't!"

Susan adjusts her pink batter's helmet. "All right, lucky first pitch. Let's see if you got another one in you, punk!"

I shoot her a curveball this time. They're coming more easily today. Susan swings wildly and winds up spinning herself like a top. Whitney helps right her and Susan adjusts her frames.

Lexi claps wildly from second base. "Good effort! Good effort!"

"Okay, I'm warmed up now," Susan says and gets into position again.

I look at Zak. He gives me the signal for another fastball. I shake my head. Let's give the girl a break. I pitch underhand, shooting it nice and slow. Susan manages to hit a ground ball. Shrieking, she races to first base and Lexi rounds second. Sam groans.

"Thank you!" Susan calls to me.

I can feel my cheeks redden. "You're welcome!"

Keith walks on to the field with his phone in his hands. I didn't realize he left the game. "I just spoke to your coach. He said you killed it at practice and if you behave yourself all season, he'll ask the scouts to come back." The group cheers wildly.

"That's great, but I mean, will we even still be here for me to play the season?" I ask, trying not to be too much of a pill.

It's a fair question and the others turn and look at Keith as well.

"I sent out my résumé for a few jobs today," he announces.

"Like at fast food places and grocery stores?" Sam asks. I don't think he's joking.

"Um, I do have a degree in biology, thank you very much, so

no, I sent them to some research labs in the area," Keith says wryly. He nudges Sam.

"Oh, right. Forgot you actually graduated college," Sam says and Lexi snorts. "Sorry."

"I figure we'll have an estate sale and sell what we don't need," Keith explains. "I listed some stuff on Craigslist and spoke to an antiques dealer about the piano." I hear Whitney inhale sharply. "Then we'll move into an apartment close to here." He scratches his head. "It's going to be tight for a while but—"

"I can babysit more and help out," Whitney interrupts him.

"Me too," Lexi offers.

"I can find a job," I find myself saying. And I mean it.

Keith slowly smiles. "Okay then. We'll make this work."

"I'd rather leave here sooner than later," Whitney says softly, kicking the grass with her sneaker. "Just rip the Band-Aid off and move on, you know?"

"I'm with Whit." Lexi puts her arm around her again. God, she's touchy-feely today. "The longer we're here, the harder it will be to leave." Sam and I nod in agreement.

"Well, that won't be a problem," Keith says evenly. "I spoke to the bank this morning and we don't have much time left anyway." Everyone's quiet. I hear the kids on the swing set next door laughing.

God, the vibe is getting depressing again. Time to move on.

"So that settles it," I say. "We're moving. Back to the game."

Keith clasps his hands. "What team am I on?"

Zak looks at me, then tosses Keith his glove. "You can take over for me."

Lexi is surprised, just like I thought she'd be. "Where are you going?"

Zak keeps walking. "To get ready."

"For what?" Lexi calls out.

He turns around and walks backward. "I have a date."

"You have a . . ." Lexi trails off when Zak just smiles and heads around the side of the house to his car to get the change of clothes we stopped to get before we came here.

Snap! It worked like a charm. Just like I thought it would.

Beyond that, I don't want to know any of the details with those two.

Lexi pushes me. "He has a date? With who?"

I pretend to be mortally wounded. I cover my chest with my arms. "I don't know."

Lexi pushes me harder and Whitney tries to pull her back. "Jason, so help me God, I will torture you!"

"Okay, okay," I say, giving in as planned. "It's with that girl from the pizza place."

"The one with the fake boobs?" Lexi cries. "What's so great about her?" Her voice is getting louder. "Why's he going out with her?"

"I'm going to go out on a limb here and say it's because she's nice to him and knows he's super hot unlike other people in this backyard," Whitney says bluntly.

It takes a lot of effort not to laugh when Lexi starts to pout.

"I noticed he's super hot," she mumbles.

"You sure don't act like you noticed," Keith responds.

"Stop self-sabotaging yourself," Sam tells her and we all look at him. "What? We learned about that in psychology class." Keith and Whitney laugh.

"Shut up," Lexi mutters and walks off the field.

I have to assume she's headed inside to talk to Zak, just like the two of us planned.

And girls say boys are dumb.

I toss the ball in the air and catch it. I can't help but grin. "Who's ready to get back to the game?"

21 //
LEXI

Zak has a date with some blonde bimbo?

Not happening. No way. *Never.*

Zak likes me!

And I . . .

I like him.

I've always liked him.

I've just been too much of an ass to admit it to myself. Why have a decent relationship in your life, Lexi? You excel at attracting losers like Jared who cheat on you and treat you like crap. Meanwhile, Zak has been standing in the wings, watching and waiting for me since God knows when. It was Zak who came to my rescue after Jared ditched me at that party and that slut laid me out. It's Zak who always has my back when something's going on here at home. He's always trying to make me remember who I really am. That pissed me off for a while . . . until I finally realized the only way to get my life back on track was to take hold of it again. And now new-old Lexi is in control again and she wants . . . Zak.

We belong together. He puts up with my shit and I can handle his sarcastic mouth. We gel like marshmallow fluff and white bread. He does not belong with that blonde at the pizza place. He belongs with me. He knows it and I know it.

Zak just wants me to say it.

I pace my bedroom, kicking clothes on the floor and pushing shoes out of the way. I stop and stand in the middle of the room, staring at the bathroom door that links my room to Jason's. I can hear Zak whistling in there while he shaves. Getting his skin nice and smooth for some other girl. I have to stop him. "I can do this." I psych myself up.

Then I hear the shower turn on.

"No, I can't," I mutter to myself.

But if I don't do it now, while I have the courage, I might never do it. I'll just keep denying what's right in front of me and lose out on the one good thing that's come out of the last year: Zak.

I have to tell him how I feel and I have to do it now. I take a deep breath and bust into the bathroom. I squint to see through the warm steam. God, this boy takes hot showers. I walk straight to the shower door, which is all fogged up, and knock on it.

He wipes away some of the fog, sees me, and jumps. "Lexi?" He covers himself with his hands, but it's too late. Wowza. Zak should definitely go shirtless more often. "Jesus, what are you doing in here?" he freaks out.

"I need to talk to you." Isn't it obvious?

His eyes widen. "Now? Kinda busy here. Kinda naked."

Who is he kidding? He's been dreaming of me walking in on him in the shower for a year. I, um, have too. I walk to the towel rack and grab a towel for him. I sling it over the top of the shower door. I can't help but smile coyly. "Then get dressed and come out here and talk to me."

"Can't this wait ten minutes?" Zak asks.

"No!" I might lose my nerve by then. I wipe my brow. Is it really hot in here or am I just freaking out? "I'm sorry, okay?" I shout over the running water.

"You're what?" Zak yells back. He turns off the water and grabs the towel.

"I said, I'm sorry," I try again, afraid to lose my nerve. "I know I've been difficult, but I've tried to be more decent the last few days."

"Decent? By barging in on my shower."

I exhale loudly and roll my eyes. "Stop making this so difficult," I snap.

Compose yourself, Lexi.

"It's complicated, okay?" I say softly and walk to the door. I hear Zak open the shower door and step out as I turn around. He's wrapped the towel around his taut waist. His dirty-blond hair is slicked back and dripping wet down his chest. The water beads on his pecs and hangs there. Geez, he's got a nice set of abs.

"Everything about this family is complicated." Zak grabs another towel and I watch him run it over his head. His hair looks cutely messy now and sticks out in all directions. I have an overwhelming urge to run my fingers through it. "That's why I'm heading home tonight. I'll be out of your hair from now on."

Wait, what did he just say? "No! You can't," I protest. I really thought just showing up in this bathroom would be enough to get his attention. It always was before. Anytime I even sneezed in his direction, he came running like a puppy to a dog biscuit. Suddenly he's grown into a German shepard and is over my tricks. "Please don't go. I don't want you to go on that date tonight either!"

Zak slowly begins to smile and I look away as he walks over to me, holding the towel firmly around his waist. Water drips from his arms and onto the floor I'm now staring at. "Oh, really?"

"Yes," I tell his feet.

"And why is that?" He presses.

God, he can be such an ass! I look into his milk chocolate–brown eyes and stumble for a moment. He's so close I could brush that water droplet off his cheek. "You're really going to make me say this?" I sound pissed. I shouldn't sound pissed.

He just keeps grinning like a Cheshire cat. "Yep, I'm going to make you say it."

I huff and stare at the tile again. I can hear the water dripping in the shower and the sound of my own heartbeat as Zak stands there in front of me half-naked waiting for me to say the things I should have said a long time ago. We've come close to kissing so many times before and I've pulled away. I don't want to be scared anymore, but it's so hard to put my feelings on the line.

Why is it so hard for me to just say it out loud? *I need you. I want you. Please don't leave me.*

"Lexi?" Zak's voice is soft and when I look at his face again, I almost close my eyes and wait for him to kiss me. "I'm waiting."

Oh. Right. I have some explaining to do. I glance away. It's too hard to concentrate when I'm staring into those big eyes of his that remind me of a cool glass of Coca-Cola. "I was afraid, okay? Everything about my life sucked this year—losing Mom, losing Dad, now losing this house. I was just so angry all the time."

He nods. "Don't I know it?"

If he keeps interrupting me, I'll lose my train of thought and then I'll never get this out. I put my hand out to shut him up and my fingers come to rest on his bare chest. Wow, that feels nice. I try to focus, even though we're both staring at my hand. Zak doesn't flinch. "Let me finish," I say softly.

"Okay." His voice comes out husky.

"I was angry and miserable ninety percent of the time and you didn't care. I tried to forget who I was before and you didn't care. I completely changed my look and you didn't care. You always saw the real me beneath the pain and you still liked me." I look into his eyes again. "I didn't think I deserved that." His eyebrows furrow. "How could I lose so much and still have such a great guy be into me? It didn't make sense. If my life sucked, it all had to suck. I know that sounds stupid, but it was easier to wallow in the pain than to accept that something good could happen to me when everything was falling apart." My fingers curl around a tuft of his chest hair. "So I pushed you away so I could keep feeling bad for myself, but I don't want to feel this hollow anymore. I want to be with you. I—"

"What took you so long?" Zak pulls me toward him and cups my face. "Get over here."

When he kisses me, any doubt I had about this being wrong washes away. His lips are softer than I imagined and his kisses are less urgent than Jared's ever were. He always seemed like he was trying to devour me whole. But Zak . . . Zak's kiss feels right and I know I don't want him to stop anytime soon. He gently lifts me up onto the vanity, and I lock my legs around his waist while we keep kissing.

Kiss me and love me, I think.

I can handle it and I'm ready for whatever comes next.

22 // WHITNEY

When the U-Haul pulls up in front of the house, I'm actually relieved.

It's time to go. I'm ready to move on. We all are. Keith found an apartment and he's got some leads on jobs. We've sold off the piano, which will cover a few months' rent, and Harry is trying to get Mom's will turned over to Keith. It's going to be okay. I know that now. We all do.

"U-Haul's here!" Sam yells as I head downstairs for one of the last times.

"Yeah, we kind of noticed," I say and jump down the final two steps like I always did as a kid. Keith is standing among the boxes of things we're bringing with us. Clothes, pictures, kitchen stuff, and only few mementos of our life here. He had us each pick out something that reminded us of home to take with us. My dollhouse won't fit in the apartment, but Keith was good enough to get Harry to put it in his attic until the day comes when I have room for it again. Who knows? Maybe it will go in my kid's room someday. For now, I'm happy with my pictures. The box of photos that came on our road trip and the shell frame with Mom and Dad's wedding picture in it. I walk over to the couch we're taking with us, and without asking, Keith and I each pick up an end and begin walking it to the front door.

"Watch the walls," Keith reminds me as we pass Jason and Zak in the hallway carrying more boxes labeled JASON'S STUFF! TROPHIES. I guess he didn't bust all of them.

"I can't believe you guys are leaving this place." Zak shakes his head. "I kind of feel like I lived here." Lexi bounds down the steps looking unbelievably cheerful for 9:00 a.m.

"You pretty much did live here," Jason says.

"True," Zak agrees. He turns to Lexi. "Hey."

"Hey," she says back and kisses him.

"Gross!" Jason sounds like Sam. "Get a room."

"I'm going to have to get used to seeing that," Keith says to me.

"Me too," I agree, but it makes me happy. If Lexi can find someone worthy, chances are I will someday too. A guy like Scott Dwyer just didn't deserve me.

Zak pulls away. "I'll see you tomorrow."

"Okay," Lexi murmurs and then she watches him walk out the front door with one of the last of Jason's boxes. She turns and takes one from the stack in the living room. "What?" she says when she catches me staring at her. I blush when I think of how I caught the two of them making out in the bathroom, Zak wet from the shower and wrapped in a bath towel from the waist down. I bolted. It was easier to let a hallucination take over and imagine them singing that Calvin Harris song "I Need Your Love."

"It's just nice to see you happy," I reply and maneuver my end of the couch successfully through the front door. Keith follows.

My sister smiles. "I know."

A few hours later, the U-Haul is packed up and the house is pretty much empty. The walls are bare except for the markings left behind by old photographs. I walk through the rooms looking for anything we might have forgotten and hear the floor creak beneath my feet. Then I meet the others outside where Keith is lowering the back gate on the truck.

"Well, that's pretty much it," he says quietly and stares back at the house.

We all look at the stately Tudor that's been our home since before I can remember. The lights are all on and you can see inside the empty rooms. It's an eerie feeling.

"I don't want to go back inside," I say. "The house doesn't feel like our own anymore."

"I feel the same way," Keith agrees, "but we don't get the apartment keys until tomorrow, so why don't we all just camp out in the living room?"

"I could handle that," I say and Lexi and Jason nod.

Sam runs to the truck where our sleeping bags are packed up. He pulls his out and begins walking back up the path. "I'm glad you said that, Keith, because there was no way I was sleeping upstairs in my room alone."

"Me neither." Lexi heads to the car to get the pillows. "It's creepy up there now."

The rest of us grab our stuff and head inside. I try not to think too much about each thing I do and how it could be the last time I do it. The last time I walk through the front door. The last time I open the fridge. The last time I knock on Susan's door to pick her up from school. (We've both agreed to just meet on the main steps now so that we can walk in together. It's not nearly as scary being apart on our walk to school now that we don't have the She-Bitches to worry about anymore.) I unroll my sleeping bag and place it on the living room floor next to the others.

"Remember when we used to do this on Christmas Eve?" I ask.

Lexi props up her pillow. "Yep. We'd wait for Santa down here and Mom and Dad would let us roast marshmallows in the fireplace."

Keith has his sleeping bag pulled up under his chin. "Pretty smart, when you think about it. All that sugar would make us crash."

"Which may explain why we never caught Santa in the act," says Sam. "In the morning, we'd wake up and . . ."

". . . and the presents would just be there under the tree," Jason finishes, his eyes on the empty wall in the corner where our tree always stood.

I can almost smell the pine needles. Mom and Dad fought over a real versus fake tree every year. Dad wanted a fake one so he could put it up the day after Thanksgiving and Mom wanted the fresh scent of a real fir and wouldn't hear of it. She always won. I'm going to try not to think about what kind of a tree we'll have in our new apartment. At least Keith kept all of our ornaments and boxed them up for storage. We're all quiet.

"I'm gonna miss this place," Lexi says, moving her sleeping bag closer to Sam's. The two of them move their pillows together so they're one.

"Me too," Jason says as Keith slides out of his sleeping bag and turns off the lights.

The room goes dark except for a beam of light from the windows from a nearby street lamp. We're all quiet again. I don't think it's later than 9:00 p.m., but there's nothing left to say. I think we all want to be alone in our thoughts and memories of this house. No one wants to say the one thing that's still on all our minds: we have to find Dad.

I don't know how long I'm lying there, remembering the time Jason and I tried to go sledding down the staircase in the front hall (Mom was not happy), when I hear what I think is a knock at the door. Keith stumbles out of his sleeping bag and I hear the others stirring. He opens the front door and squints at the brightness from the porch light.

"Harry? What's going on?" Keith's voice is sleepy.

"Can we come in?" I hear him say.

We?

I sit straight up and Lexi jumps up to turn on the overhead lights. I feel kind of silly sitting on the floor in my pajamas in a sleeping bag, but Harry doesn't say anything about it as he walks in with a police officer right behind him. Sam and Jason scramble out of their sleeping bags. We all stand together on the side of the room, and I get a sinking feeling in the pit of my stomach. *Why does Harry have a cop with him?* We're allowed to be here till tomorrow, I think. At least that's what Keith told us.

"Maybe you should tell them," Harry says to the officer who nods.

The policeman looks at us. "We found your father." My stomach does a backflip.

Lexi's mouth hangs open, and Jason puts an arm around her. His face is stoic. Sam grabs my hand and bounces up and down on his toes excitedly, but I'm not that optimistic. If they found Dad and he's not here, where is he?

"You found our dad?" Keith asks, his voice eager. "Where?" He looks from Harry to the cop. "When?"

"Last night." The officer is hesitant. He removes his cap and looks around the room at all of us in our pajamas. "I'm afraid it's not good news."

I knew it. "Oh God." I sink down onto the floor and Jason puts a hand on my shoulder.

"There was a storm several months back—" the officer starts to explain.

"—The night Dad left," I tell the others. Their faces are now a mix of bewilderment and worry.

"City workers were out fixing some downed power lines in the hills yesterday," the officer continues. "They were off the beaten path, so it took a while to get to." He looks at Keith. "They came across a car that had been hit. It looks like it ran through the guardrails and crashed at the bottom of the ravine. It probably happened the night of the storm." He clears his throat and says the words I'm dreading. "We identified the driver as your father. I'm sorry."

Sam starts to pace and his arms are flailing wildly. I can practically see his heart beating out of his chest. "He's dead?" His voice is panicked. "You're saying our dad is dead?"

Keith pulls Sam into a bear hug. "It's okay; it's okay," he repeats, stroking Sam's head. It sounds like he's trying to reassure himself as well. "Did he . . . did he suffer?"

"No," the officer says. "We believe he died on impact. We think he hit a deer and lost control."

My head is spinning. I watch as the room around me begins to flip and I feel like I'm standing on the ceiling. I get a sour taste in my mouth and then begin to see colors. I know a hallucination will take over any minute now and I have to stop it for just a little while longer. I stand up again. There's something I need to know. "Do you know in what direction he was headed?"

"From what we can tell, it seems like he was headed back here," the cop responds and looks at Harry. "The gas station attendant nearby remembered him once we showed him the photograph. He said your dad didn't want to wait out the rain. He wanted to get back to his kids."

That's all I had to hear. I burst into tears and Lexi pats my back. It's almost overwhelming hearing all this, but at the same time, it's strangely comforting too. "So he never left us?" I say to myself as well as the others. "All this time we've been hating him and blaming him and he never left us. He just went for a drive and got in an accident on the way back."

Tears are streaming down Sam's face. Lexi leans her head into Jason's and starts to cry. Jason stays strong, but I know he's holding back tears. Keith just looks stunned.

"I know you probably don't care about this at the moment," Harry says quietly, "but your dad had a two-million-dollar life insurance police." He puts his arm on Keith's shoulder. "You're going to be fine now. Keith, you'll have access to all of it. I'll call the bank in the morning and will sort out the mortgage. You won't have to move."

Keith exhales deeply and runs a hand through his hair. His eyes are watery. "Thanks, Harry."

Harry seems reluctant to take his hand off Keith's shoulder, but he finally does and seems to realize we need some time to process all this. "I'll check on you guys later." He closes the door behind him, but nobody moves.

We all just stand where we were, unsure of what to do next. My thoughts come fast and furious as sparks of red, blue, and green flash in front of my eyes.

Dad didn't leave us. He loved us. He was in an accident. All this time we thought he abandoned ship, but he didn't. He was coming home to us this whole time. But now that will never happen.

I let out a sob and cover my mouth. "I just need to be alone." I run upstairs before anyone can stop me. Out of the corner of my eye, I see Lexi, Sam, and Jason sink back onto their sleeping bags.

"Me too." I hear Keith say and he opens the front door again.

Upstairs, I flip on the lights and the empty hall transforms into a movie screen. Ever since we got back from the road trip, I've been trying to fight the hallucinations more and live in the moment. But after news like this, I let the side effects fully take over again. Images of my father flicker in front of me and I feel drawn to them. The first one leads me to a window at the end of the hallway. When I look out into the moonlight, I see Keith leaning against the den wall where he thinks none of us can see him. He's just standing there, and then he breaks down. I walk away to give him some privacy. Below me, I know Jason and Sam must be doing the same thing. I blink back my own tears and wipe my face. I need a song to get through this moment. "Without You" by David Guetta seems fitting because the words are so true. I have no idea how I'm going to make it through life without my father.

A memory of Jason and my dad runs by me in the empty hall. They're both in baseball uniforms and Dad is tossing Jason a ball before one of their games. I walk a little farther and see Sam riding piggyback on Dad. The two of them seem to be laughing. I look out another window and see Lexi and my father doing cartwheels together. They both come out of their cartwheels and fall down laughing. Nearby, I see the image of Keith and Dad having a heart-to-heart on the garden bench the two of them built together.

When I reach the staircase landing again, I see a younger me dressed up for a school dance. Dad is taking my picture. I pose dramatically for him. The image fades and the front door seemingly opens. I watch as Dad walks through it. Tall, strong, with salt-and-pepper hair and dark eyes, he looks up at me and smiles that superwhite grin of his.

"How are we going to go on without you?" I cry out to his ghost.

Dad smiles at me sadly. "You already have," he seems to say and then he fades away.

He's right. We've been going on ever since the day he disappeared. Yes, it's been hell, it's been scary, and there have been days none of us have wanted to go on, but we're still here. I wish none of this ever happened, but there's no denying we're stronger than we were six months ago. If that road trip proved anything, it's that you can't keep a Connolly down. We're a team and if we stick together, we're going to be fine. Isn't that what Dad always said when he taught each of us how to swim?

"You don't need me to hold you anymore, Whitney Connolly," he'd say, giving me a shove and pushing me out in the middle of the deep end where it was either sink or swim. "You're going to be fine on your own."

The memory leads me to the backyard and the pool. I'm not surprised to find Lexi, Sam, and Jason already there, standing at the edge, looking into the still water. Moonlight bounces off the water and reflects our images back at us. I see Keith's come into view and know he's behind me. We look strong standing together like this. I stare at the water again and see our younger selves in the pool with Mom and Dad. We're playing Marco Polo. Jason is it and Dad keeps tossing Sam in his direction. We're all splashing and screaming and having a great time. Dad may be gone, but I don't need a hallucination to know that no one can take away our memories.

Lexi and I look at each other. She grabs my hand. Keith takes the other one and then he reaches out for Sam. Jason takes Lexi's other hand. The five of us look at each other and then without a word, we jump into the icy water, fully clothed. Our shrieking will probably wake the neighbors, but who cares. We don't live here anymore. Oh wait. We still can live here.

I wipe the water away from my face and look at Keith as I tread water. "I don't want to stay here. It's too hard."

"She's right," Lexi agrees emphatically. "We need a fresh start. Everywhere I turn, I see Dad. I see Mom. I see how it used to be and it's just too hard to relive the past day in and day out."

Jason bobs up and down. "And Keith, you shouldn't have to give up on med school to take care of us. Mom and Dad wouldn't want you to either." The rest of us mumble in agreement.

Keith pulls himself out of the water and offers Sam a hand. The rest of us begin to get out. The air is cool and I feel a chill run down my back, but I'm not ready to go back in that house. I'd almost rather sleep in the car.

"Are you guys sure?" Keith asks. "I was thinking about trying to transfer to somewhere close to here so I could keep up a few classes."

"No," Sam says firmly. "We all leave. Together."

"We'll move back with you to UC San Diego." I start thinking. "It's only a few hours from here and we can still visit our friends."

Lexi twists a strand of hair around her finger and smiles. "I've always wanted to live in a college town." The rest of us groan.

"God help us all," Keith says.

"Zak will keep her in line," Jason tells us. "He's already been accepted to UCSD next year."

"Who are we kidding?" Keith asks. "Knowing Zak, he'll probably move in with us there too." Everyone laughs. In the distance, a dog barks. Keith looks at us. "Are you guys sure about this?" His voice can't hide his excitement. "All of you?"

We nod in agreement. "This isn't our home anymore," I say. "It's time we move on."

Keith puts his arm around me. "Okay. It's settled. The Connollys are moving to San Diego." Sam hollers and Jason claps. This is really happening. "The U-Haul's packed. I say we head straight there tomorrow and call Harry on the way and tell him our plan. There's always housing near campus. We'll find a place, enroll you guys in a school with a great ball team, and hell, if we can't find a house tomorrow, at least now we have the money to stay at a hotel till we do."

"No more camping," Lexi insists and I laugh.

"Deal," Keith says and we all put our hands in a circle and give a little team cheer.

That's what we forgot this year. We're a team and it's going to stay that way from now on.

No one gets much sleep. We spend half the night talking and making plans. Lexi is on the phone with Zak, telling him the news the minute we get back to the living room. I text Susan and fill her in on our plan. She says she'll get her mom to take her down to see me next weekend. This is going to work.

———•———

As the sun streams through the living room windows the next morning, we roll up our sleeping bags and start heading to the car. It's a beautiful morning for a fresh start. I start to hum the lyrics to "Burn" sung by Ellie Goulding because the thought of not worrying about the future anymore is very appealing. Lexi looks at me and realizes I'm humming. Then she surprises me by humming along. We smile at each other and that's when I remember. "I forgot something inside. I'll be right back."

I race back through the house for the last time, not stopping to let the ghosts of the past pay a visit. I go straight to my bathroom and stare at my reflection in the cabinet mirror. Then I open the door and see the familiar orange bottle with the white cap that has been my BF (no offense Susan) for the last six months.

But not anymore.

I untwist the cap and see there's one lone pill left. I take a deep breath and turn on the faucet. Then I dump the pill into the sink. I watch as the water claims the pill and it circles the drain.

I hear the front door open. "Whit? You okay?" Keith asks.

I look at my face in the mirror and smile before turning back to the door and shutting off the light. "I'm fine!"

And for the first time in a long time, it's the truth.

I'm fine now, and I'm ready for whatever this life throws at me next.

JEN CALONITA is the author of many young adult novels, including *Summer State of Mind* and the Secrets of My Hollywood Life series. *Secrets*, which is about a teen TV star on the rise, was inspired by her job as an entertainment editor at a teen magazine where she interviewed everyone from Justin Timberlake to Zac Efron.

Jen invites you to visit her online at www.jencalonitaonline.com and on Twitter @jencalonita

READ ON FOR AN EXCERPT FROM

AWESOMENESS TV

R U N A W A Y S

by BETH SZYMKOWSKI

based on the series created by
BETH SZYMKOWSKI

ALSO AVAILABLE NOW FROM

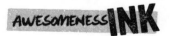

PROLOGUE

Olivia Abernathy stood staring down at the closed trunk of her husband's white Mercedes. Dark streaks of blood marred the otherwise pristine surface.

It was not what she'd expected to find when she woke that morning and found his side of the bed empty. Again.

She'd risen with the grace of the dancer she once was, a ballerina with plans to tour the world on her toes until she fell for William Abernathy IV. He was a gorgeous playboy from a wealthy family, accustomed to money solving all the problems his fast living created. When he smiled, her dreams and everything else fell away.

She'd dressed and made her way to the kitchen, where she poured a finger of orange juice into the cut-glass tumbler, then added vodka to the rim before gulping it down. Breakfast of champions. The sting in her throat was familiar and soothing. It wouldn't be long before her body would warm and relax from its effects.

She grabbed her keys and made for the garage. Inside, she was surprised to see William's car in his parking spot next to hers. If he didn't sleep in their bed and hadn't gone anywhere in his car, where was he? She'd moved to look inside the frosted windows when . . .

WHAM! Her feet flew out from under her. Her head bounced on the concrete floor. She floundered, trying to right herself, but the floor was slick with something and the more she moved, the more she slipped. Finally, she pulled herself up, taking care like she would if she were standing on ice. She inhaled deeply, regaining her composure, and stared down at her white shift dress.

It was covered in bright red blood.

Olivia fought the scream that was rising fast like bile in her throat. She clenched her mouth shut and told herself to hold it together. She was not a screamer. She was calm in a crisis. It was one of her better qualities. Her ability to remain unruffled in difficult situations was the reason the Danbury Country Club's social chair was always calling her when things were falling apart.

But a sizable pool of blood on the garage floor was definitely different than trouble with an overwhelmed caterer or temperamental florist. Olivia focused on her breathing and stared at the dark puddle. It was large and extended to underneath the back of William's car. Someone had dragged something or someone to his trunk.

What the hell had happened? William had made his share of enemies in the business world and had a remarkably relative sense of personal ethics, but he'd never been involved in anything violent. Violence was ugly and he was anything but.

When a car drove by outside, Olivia moved into action. She couldn't allow the occupants to see her soiled dress or the slick, red floor. She quickly closed the garage door, realizing what she did next would be dictated by what she found inside the trunk. She braced herself, staring at the closed lid.

Ordinarily, it would be empty, save for the built-in jack and spare tire and maybe William's golf clubs. He was very fastidious that way. He liked things to feel unused and got a new car every two years, as soon as the new-car smell wore off. Olivia was the opposite. While she obviously always drove a luxury vehicle, and wouldn't drive anything more than five years old, she detested having to learn all the bells and whistles of a new ride. She wanted to know how to turn on the windshield wipers without thinking about it. It was typical of their differences. William had always been looking for things to entertain him, much like a child wanting an endless supply of new toys. Luckily, he had a generous trust fund to support his needs. He also worked and appeared to be successful, but Olivia knew his earnings could never support his lifestyle.

She couldn't put it off much longer. She needed to open the damn thing and see what, or who, was inside.

Her hand shook as she pressed the button on the car remote. She braced herself as the trunk slowly opened. Given the size of the bloodstain on the garage floor, she felt certain whoever, or whatever, was in the trunk would be a particularly gruesome sight. She let out a slow exhalation when she saw no signs of the mayhem that had to have occurred, but only the shape of a body wrapped in blankets and sheets.

She took a broom from where it leaned nearby and poked the pile with the handle, not sure what would happen. She half expected somebody to pop up and yell, "Boo!" The thought oddly amused her.

She poked again. Nothing. She tried again, this time firmly pressing the wood into the mound. A red spot appeared, flowering as the wetness spread into a large crimson stain.

Taking another breath, Olivia pulled back the covers to see whom William had killed.

1. MASON AND KAYLEE ARE MISSING

Trevor Anthony sat with a handful of students in the sun-dappled hallway outside the Danbury Prep administrative offices, waiting to be questioned by the police. The grave faces of past Danbury leaders stared down at them from photos lining the wall.

The students gathered were an unusual mix, from one of the oddest girls in school to the class president. Trevor thought of himself as the class eunuch. He was popular with the girls because of his polished style and sharp wit, but, of course, he never had a relationship with any of them. Their parts didn't match the way he wanted them to.

Keesha Washington spoke first. That was typical. Keesha was usually the first one to raise her hand in class. Always straight up, like she was raising a signal flag. "Kaylee didn't come to first period," she said. Keesha and Kaylee had been best friends since the beginning of freshman year three years ago. She was a bit hurt that Kaylee clearly was involved in something major and she knew nothing about it, but Keesha wasn't about to show her feelings to anyone else. She always behaved in a professional manner. Her long auburn hair was tucked behind her ears, revealing dainty pearl earrings.

"Mason wasn't there either," added Glinda Adams. Glinda, on the other hand, was all about flash. Everything about her called attention to herself. She wore an assortment of seven-inch platform shoes and had long blonde hair tinted green near the ends: the perfect complement to her prep-school plaid skirt and blazer, of course.

Mason Henry and Kaylee Abernathy were the most controversial couple at the school. She was a well-liked cheerleader and he was a charity case with a perpetual chip on his shoulder. People either delighted in the inherent romance of such a mismatch or took bets on how long before it flamed out. Glinda gave them three months max. But even she had no idea it would end with authorities involved.

"I don't see why we had to get called out of class to answer questions about them cutting." Keesha shook her head. "If I miss my Orgo test and all she did was ditch, Kaylee will be so sorry."

"Please. Tell me you don't think we're all being interrogated because two people cut class?" Lily Mars was annoyed. "I thought this school was supposed to cater to society's elite, not society's imbecilic."

"Is that even a word?" asked Keesha. "My point is that something bigger is going on," Lily glared at her.

"She's right," said Glinda. "Cutting is not a crime for the cops."

"Does anybody care what you think?" Lily shot Glinda a withering look. She didn't care if she was agreeing with her; at no point was the little toad to think they were on friendly terms together.

Lily was the de facto social leader of the school. Glinda was a loser. The fact that they were sitting anywhere near each other and were engaged in the same discussion was remarkable. Glinda was well aware of the social divides and that she was crossing them. She smiled sweetly at Lily and batted her eyes.

"People are saying they ran away." Keesha crossed her ankles and folded her hands in her lap. Rumors were flying fast through everyone's phones. One chain of texts had Mason withdrawing a large sum of money at an ATM near the Canadian border and another had them both spotted at the airport waiting to board a flight to Belize. Keesha knew that was wrong. Kaylee had been to Belize and hated the humidity.

"I heard Kaylee's room was messed up," Trevor said to no one in particular. He was worried. Kaylee had been extremely upset last night, and he hoped she hadn't done anything irrational.

"So's mine," Glinda mused.

"Why doesn't that surprise me?" Lily shook her head. What the hell was she doing here?

"Kaylee's usually neat. Weirdly neat." Trevor considered that a compliment. Kaylee was one of the few people Trevor would ever consider living with because they shared an aversion to clutter.

Senior class president Jared Slater spoke for the first time. He'd been pacing, unable to hold his long and muscular body still. "Who cares how clean her room was? How can that be relevant?"

"Because if it's been ransacked, that means something happened," Keesha explained.

"Or if it's just slightly messy, maybe she packed in a hurry and then ran away." Trevor's mind was racing.

Neither idea sat well with Jared. He had dated Kaylee briefly a few months ago but then she broke up with him. He never stopped liking her. Jared was dismayed she ended up with a thug like Mason and thought she was crying out for help in some way. When she was ready to date someone more appropriate, he planned to take her back without holding any of her bad choices against her. He refused to believe she would run away with Mason. Even cutting wasn't like Kaylee. She was one of the good girls.